SAN DIEGO RAYS SERIES

SIN & WAR

GINSA MICHELLE
GRAYCE RIAN

Contents

DEDICATION

To everyone who sat back, watched the men in tight baseball pants slap each other's asses, and secretly wondered if their favorite players would ever kiss.
We give you: Sin & War.

CONTENT NOTE

Dear Readers,

While the two of us do not have the lived experiences of Will and Brooks, we wanted to take great care in accurately portraying their lives as individuals in the queer community. We're so thankful to our sensitivity reader for providing feedback and guidance for Will and Brooks' stories as bi-sexual men.

This book contains mature themes and potentially triggering content, including on-page explicit sex and language, loss of a family member (off-page), recreational alcohol use, on-page disconcerting situations, internal homophobia and fear of external homophobia, past homophobic violence against a main character (off-page), past childhood trauma, unprotected sex, and exhibitionism. Despite being a romance novella with a happy ever after, readers should be aware of these themes.

xx,
Ginsa & Grayce

SAN DIEGO RAYS ROSTER:

#11 — William "Sin" Sinclair — Pitcher

#99 — Brooks "War" Warren — Catcher

#3 — Mateo "Mat" Costa — Shortstop

#21 — Truett "Ham" Embers — First Baseman

#67 — Renji "Ren" Sakamoto — Second Baseman

#8 — Graham "Graham Cracker/Lenny" Lennox — Third Baseman / Relief Catcher

#45 — Joel "Cruzer" Cruz — Center Fielder

#36 — Bembe "Bebe" Batista — Right Fielder

#14 — Lucas "Lefty" Milner — Left Fielder

#22 — Shane "Hughesy" Hughes — Relief Pitcher

Coach: Quentin Hunter

Pitching Coach: Frank Adams

PROLOGUE

WILL - FUCKING SAN DIEGO

EIGHTY-EIGHT. EIGHTY-NINE. NINETY.

My phone rings incessantly off to the side of my mat where I'm finishing the hundred pushups I complete every morning.

Ninety-seven. Ninety-eight.

The ringing starts again, and I grind through the final two pushups before standing up and swiping to accept my agent's phone call.

"Jerry, this better be good; you know I don't like to begin my day on the phone," I tell him, slightly breathless from the exertion.

"Good morning to you too, William. I would think after nine calls, you'd realize it's important."

"I was finishing my workout. What's up?" I ask as I turn the TV on mute and swipe my sports drink off my kitchen island.

"There's no easy way to say this, Will, but you've been traded."

Sputtering and coughing, I nearly choke mid-sip. "You're fucking with me."

"Afraid not."

My chest squeezes in panic. "Why the fuck are you the one telling me?"

"Front office thought it'd come better from me."

More like my father couldn't nut up and call me himself. But why would the almighty Jameson Sinclair call his oldest son to inform him he'd traded him to a different team?

"To which team?" I growl out the question.

"San Diego," he informs me, and my stomach drops.

"I'm sorry, could you repeat that? It sounded like you said San Diego, which can't be right because they're one of the worst teams in the league, and I'm one of the best fucking starting pitchers in the game right now."

Jerry sighs on the other end of the line. "Will, be that as it may, you're nearing retirement, and you of all people should know how this works."

"Considering I've been with St. Louis for the past eight seasons after signing a ten-year deal, I'm not sure why I'd know how this works. I've never been traded. I signed with Philly out of college and then signed with St. Louis after my rookie contract was up. Seeing as you're my agent, I didn't think I needed to remind you of that," I say like a complete asshole.

"You didn't have a no-trade clause in your contract—"

I cut him off, shouting, "Because I didn't think I'd fucking have to considering I signed with my own family's team!"

"I'm sorry, Will, but what's done is done." He breathes out a sigh of frustration. "You're to report to San Diego in two days for your first practice. I've booked you a short-term rental until you find a place to get settled. Pack what you can today, and I'll get the movers to your place first thing in the morning."

"Is that all?" I ask, not waiting for him to answer before hanging up.

Slamming my phone on the counter, I run my fingers through my hair and shut my eyes.

In the back of my mind, I always knew this day would come. For whatever reason, I just thought I could finish my career playing in a city I love for a team I've spent nearly the past decade playing for.

Instead, I'll be reporting to play for the San Diego Rays in two days.

Needing to clear my mind, I pick up my phone and open Instagram, only to be enraged once again. The Rays' profile is filled with reels of the team jacking around. They won't have a shot at making the playoffs if they don't start taking things seriously.

Gritting my teeth, I curse my father for trading me to this godforsaken group of degenerates.

1
BROOKS

When Sin Walks In

I LET THE COOL water from the shower rain over my head, squeezing my eyes shut as it runs in rivulets down my face. I'm the last one to get a shower after my strength training session ran over.

My ears strain to listen to the commotion around me. I hear bits and pieces of heated conversation mixed with laughter. I pay no mind until I make out the word "traded," and I quickly shut the water off and grab my towel from the hook.

"Coach confirmed it. It's happening." I hear our shortstop, Mateo Costa talking to our first baseman, Truett Embers.

"What's happening?" I ask, situating myself in front of my locker while the others slowly gather around Mateo.

"Coach brought on your new boy toy, War," Mateo teases. I ignore his quip and dig for more.

"Someone got traded?"

"*Sí*. The one and only Will Sinclair."

I huff out a laugh, tugging my towel off to slip on a fresh pair of briefs.

Will Sinclair. Mateo couldn't be further from the truth. Will isn't my type. He's way too stiff for my taste. He's the perfect, nepo pretty boy bachelor whose daddy owns the St. Louis Bullfrogs—the team we absolutely loathe here in Rays nation. His family is known as MLB royalty as well, going back generations within the organization.

Must be nice.

I'm surprised he's getting traded from a team he's been playing on almost his entire career. I wonder what the deal is with knowing Daddy Sinclair willingly allowed management to trade his son.

But Sinclair is too clean cut for me to play with. I like my men rough around the edges and my women soft with a mouth that can suck like a Hoover. Plus, the man was born with a trust fund that will set his great grandkids up for life. He's never had to work a day in his existence outside of his baseball career. I'll give him credit for his talent, but the man was born with a silver spoon holding his mashed peas. He can fuck right off.

"Funny, Costa. It seems you don't know me at all. Sinclair seems more your type. You know, arrogant, pompous dicks. You're a match made in heaven."

Laughter erupts from around the locker room, and Mateo flips me off. I return the sentiment, giving him a kissy face for good measure.

"The guy is on his last legs in the league," I chide. "That arrogance comes with his old age, boys."

"I don't know, War. He's thirty-four, not ninety," Truett cuts in, a playful grin tugging his lips. "Although, come to think of it, you could probably use an older man to put you in your place. God knows you need it."

"Sinclair is ten years older than you and could probably run circles around your ass, *papi*," Mateo tacks on.

Fists bang on lockers and loud laughter echoes off the walls from my teammates, all at my expense. Whatever. Even though I'm trying to whip anyone within a foot of me with my towel, I love these guys no matter how much shit they throw my way.

"Old and arrogant, huh?"

A deep voice cuts through the laughter, and a set of deep blue eyes are suddenly on me. The scowl on his face should agitate me, but the complete opposite happens, throwing me a curve ball I didn't see coming.

Will Sinclair is fucking hot.

I don't miss the fullness of his lips, the sharp edge of his strong jaw, and those eyes. Those beautiful, navy eyes that hold so much mystery. I find my tongue darting out to wet my lips because they've suddenly gone bone dry at the sight of him.

He's leaning on the edge of the door frame from where he entered, his biceps bulging from the way he's crossing his arms across his firm chest that imprints through the white dress shirt he's wearing with the sleeves rolled up to expose his sinewy forearms. They're tan from hours in the sun, and the corded muscles flex when he reaches up to adjust the silver watch on his wrist. It looks expensive as fuck as it glints under the light.

He's paired his dress shirt with a set of perfectly tailored slacks that match his eyes to the hue, hugging his strong thighs, then tapering down toward a pair of toffee brown brogues. A smug smile tilts my lips.

Ha. Fucking pretty boy, alright.

I'm aware I'm fully checking him out, allowing my gaze to devour every gorgeous inch of his tall frame. He must be 6'3" or 6'4", almost a head taller than I am. When he runs a strong hand through his sandy blond hair, looking every bit the All-American boy he is, I shut my mouth closed before an embarrassing amount of drool leaks out, clearing my throat when he walks towards me.

"Sinclair. Welcome to San Diego. A bit overdressed, don't you think?" My eyebrow lifts, and his eyes dart down to my naked chest. I don't make any moves to put clothes on. I'm standing toe-to-toe with the enemy. I won't let this asshole intimidate me on my own turf, even if he is too pretty for his own good and has me sporting a half-chub.

"You're in California now. Loosen your collar a bit and relax. Maybe some of that *arrogance* I was talking about earlier will disappear."

This asswipe has the audacity to laugh in my face. I hate myself for the way my stomach flips when he smiles. If I could punch myself in the gut right now, I would.

"You have no room to talk shit. Brooks Warren, right?" I say nothing. He takes a half step closer, and I can feel his breath fan against my damp skin. My lips twitch to fight a smile.

"I think you boys relax a little too much here in California. It shows in the fucking rankings. So I suggest you shut the hell up and let me be as *arrogant* as I want. You can talk shit to me when your batting average improves. Until then, leave my name out of your mouth." Will seethes, then turns quickly on his heel, stomping out of the locker room.

Well, damn. That shouldn't make me horny but it does. I feel Truett snap a towel against my ass, and we all burst out laughing.

"Pretty boy tore you a new one, War. Maybe he's your type after all." Truett smirks, slapping my shoulder before leaving out the door Sinclair slammed on me.

I shake my head with a chuckle, throwing on my worn Rays hoodie and a pair of loose sweats. Slinging my bag over my shoulder, I replay the interaction between me and the new pitcher with the stormy navy eyes.

As I walk through the parking lot, finally settling in my truck, a wide smile cracks my face. I sure as fuck hope William Sinclair has more to say to me. I'm already thinking of how I'm going to grind his gears the next time I see him.

Can't fucking wait.

2

WILLIAM

This Means War

I'VE SPENT THE BETTER part of my life on a baseball diamond, and regardless of where it is, I never feel more at home than I do when my cleats are in the sand. Smoothing my fingers over the laces of the ball, I throw it back to my new teammate with a bit more speed. With each throw, a sense of calm that I haven't felt since I got the news of my trade two days ago washes over me.

"What's the deal with Warren?" I ask Shane "Hughesy" Hughes, one of our relief pitchers, as we toss a ball back and forth, warming up our arms.

"War? What do you mean?"

"I mean, he seems to have an issue with me, yet I've never done anything to him except strike him out." I pause to chuckle at the realization that he's never gotten a hit off of me in the years we've faced each other. "And yeah, I guess I beamed him last season too. But baseball aside, I've never done anything to him personally. Does he always have a stick up his ass?"

Hughesy shrugs before throwing the ball back to me. "Pretty sure he's not a fan of the upper class."

I scoff at that. "He's a professional athlete. Almost all of us are in the upper class. Especially if you've been in the league as long as I have."

"I think it has more to do with how you grew up."

"So he hates me for who my family is?" I scoff, insulted and slightly outraged.

"I doubt War hates—"

"Who do I hate?" Brooks asks, his rough voice washing over me perturbingly, which has me feathering my jaw.

And there he is as if the devil himself conjured him. Brooks Warren.

He takes off the sunglasses that were shielding his hazel eyes and then slants his black brows at me in question.

When neither of us responds, Brooks closes the distance between us, getting in my face so we're toe-to-toe like we were yesterday. Polluting the air around us, I'm hit with his notable scent—a mix of the salty ocean breeze and the sharp tang of sweat, with just a hint of coconut from his sunscreen. He narrows his uniquely mossy gaze, one leaning more toward green with amber flecks than any other hazel eyes I've come across, before he repeats himself.

Mossy gaze? Amber flecks? What the fuck is happening to me right now?

A cocky smirk lifts the corner of his mouth, exposing a deep dimple on his left cheek. "Don't be shy now, Pretty Boy. Come on, tell me. Who do I hate?"

Something is unnerving about the way he's looking at me like he can see right through my carefully constructed facade.

Clearing my throat, I answer, "Me. You seem to have a problem with me."

His answering chuckle is menacing. "Who knew you had the beauty and brains, Sin?"

"So you admit you do have a problem with me?"

"Hmm." He hums and acts as if he's mulling it over. "Is that what I said?"

"Said, no. But you implied it. And you've shown it during the few interactions we've had thus far."

Brooks waggles his brows, and his smirk grows wider. "Taking notes of all our secret meetings?"

"What the fuck?" I can't stop my face from scrunching up in disgust.

What the hell is the deal with this guy?

Before I get a chance to correct him, our pitching coach, Coach Adams, hollers at us, "Warren. Sinclair. Pull your heads outta your asses and focus!"

I step back just as Brooks turns on his heel to resume his warmup with the other catchers. Even the way he walks away is cocky and self-assured, with his jet-black hair curling out the back of his baseball hat and his batting gloves tucked into the back of his white baseball pants, bouncing with each step he takes.

A slight smile pulls at my lips thinking about yesterday. I have to admit, it was fun putting him in his place when I toured the facilities and squared away paperwork with management.

He can call me pretty boy and arrogant all he wants, but he's the one with an inflated ego, though, considering his current batting average is sitting just barely above 200, I'm not sure how. This team is a disgrace, and *War* is a contributing factor to their downward spiral.

I'd say it's about time I show my new teammates what hard work, dedication, and focus look like. Starting with War.

3

BROOKS

JEALOUS OF A HOT DOG

I'M DOING A SHIT job tossing this frisbee with Truett. Every time it leaves my hand, it flies at an alarming speed toward the heads of stray children running through Balboa Park.

"Jesus, War! Aren't you a ball player? You're shit at this!" Truett calls out, laughing as he jogs up the hill toward me.

"Watch your mouth, Ham! There're fucking kids around!"

"I don't know what's worse. You yelling 'fuck' or calling me 'Ham' in front of these innocent children." Truett gasps with his hand to his chest before smacking the side of my head with the hard plastic frisbee.

"Okay perv. The kids don't know the meaning behind your nickname, fuckface." I try my hardest to nut-check him, both of us laughing under our breaths and dodging a knee to the goods.

"Embers! War!" Coach Hunter's booming voice sobers us quickly, straightening ourselves out from our horseplay. "Could you two for five minutes not act like children? Embers, go help Hughesy with the hot dogs. I need a minute with Brooks."

Fuck.

My mind replays everything I've done or said since the last time I saw Coach, coming up short on what I could've done to earn this one-on-one with him.

Truett gives Coach a mock salute, then walks over to Hughesy, who is currently burning the hot dogs.

"Who the hell let Hughesy behind the grill? Did we not learn from last year's debacle, Coach?"

Hughesy insisted on grilling the hot dogs for the Rays' annual Memorial Day team barbecue last year. It was a massive mistake since he almost burned down half the damn park, families screaming in fear when the grill caught on fire. I mean, how the fuck does that even happen? We're lucky the fire department didn't permanently ban us.

I'm pretty sure Coach paid them off with season tickets. Smart man.

He shakes his head, dismissing my question before clearing his throat. "I need you to be on your best behavior when it comes to Sinclair."

I scrunch my nose in disgust. "The stiff? Oh, come on, Coach. He fucking hates this team. He hates this city. Why the hell should I play nice with that pretty boy?" I obviously don't share with him that Will Sinclair has been the face behind my alone time with my right hand—but I digress.

"War," he warns, "he's your pitcher. You'll be working closely together, and I'm sick of losing. This trade couldn't have worked out any better, so when I tell you to get your ass in order and take care of your new teammate, I mean it."

Well, he's right about one thing. I hate losing, and we haven't had the best season. But playing nice with Sinclair?

"Quentin! You have a phone call." Both of us whip our heads toward the direction of Stormy Hunter, Coach's smoking hot wife. We don't see her a ton with all the traveling, but she's at almost every home game, turning the heads of the entire MLB. If the WAGs had a queen, Stormy Hunter is it.

"Whoever it is, I'll call them back. I'm in the middle of an important conversation," Coach calls back with a hint of annoyance in his tone.

Weird.

Stormy rolls her eyes, turning her back with a snarky hair flip. When I turn back to Coach, his expression is more tense than before he came to probably chew my ass out.

I stir the pot, because I just can't help myself.

"Trouble in paradise there, eh Coach?" I cross my arms over my chest with a cunning smirk.

Coach Hunter's neck flames red, his jaw clenched so tight you can hear the grinding of his teeth. Steam practically smokes out of his ears, and I've thoroughly pissed him off.

God, I'm such a sucker for punishment. In more ways than one, apparently.

"Okay, Brooks. Since you want to meddle in my personal relationships and be a total dickwad, I'm assigning Sinclair to be your roommate while we're on the road."

My eyes blow wide as saucers. *What did you expect, War?* Mess with the bull and you get the horns. In this case, Coach's horns, which he shoved straight up my ass. And not in a good way.

"What?! Damn, Coach, you're killing me."

"I need you to make it right. Now go over there and be a good example for our organization. I won't have my team acting like a bunch of ass hats just because of some new blood."

Hanging my head, I blow out a relenting breath, looking over Coach Hunter's shoulder where I find a lonesome Will nursing a beer by himself at a picnic table. My heart stutters when his eyes meet mine, and I suddenly feel bad seeing him all alone.

"Yes, sir," I mutter.

Coach Hunter claps a firm hand on my shoulder, causing me to wince from the force of it.

Note to self: Shut the fuck up about Coach and his wife.

"Good on you, War. Enjoy the picnic."

Will takes his eyes off me, tracking a kite floating in the sky. He doesn't look at me at first when I take a seat across from him, his attention immersed at the kite above.

"Sinclair," I announce, watching him take a long pull from his beer before meeting my gaze.

"War." He says my name with a velvety texture, instantly making me hard beneath my jeans. To make things worse, he takes a bite from a semi-burnt hot dog, his eyes locking on mine as he does. A bit of ketchup smears on the corner of his lip, and I'm tempted to lean forward and lick it off him. I've never been jealous of a hot dog before. I watch his throat move as he swallows, and I imagine running my tongue along the length of it.

I discreetly adjust myself, not surprised he has this effect on me no matter how hard I deny it.

"I, uh. I think we got off on the wrong foot. We're going to be working together, and I promise you we aren't a bunch of degenerates like you think."

He scoffs, rolling his eyes at me like I'm bullshitting him. I lift my eyebrow in amusement, leaning closer to him, propping my elbows on the table.

"Look. I'm extending an olive branch. I'm not a bad guy, and I think you'll like having me close."

He crosses his arms over his chest as if to put a barrier between us. It only makes me want him more.

"Is that so? Or are you just playing nice because Coach Hunter told you to?" A playful smirk appears on his lips, and if the sun wasn't already making me sweat, Will Sinclair would have me in a puddle.

"Trust me. I'm about to be your favorite person." Temptation takes over as I lean across the tabletop into his space, using the pad of my thumb to wipe the ketchup from the corner of his lip. He tracks me the entire time, eyes widening slightly when I suck my ketchup-covered thumb into my mouth.

"You're a cocky shit. Aren't you, War?"

"No. I wouldn't say that. But I am *very* confident, Pretty Boy."

He huffs out a laugh, flashing two rows of straight white teeth that set my insides on fire.

"Okay. If telling yourself that helps you sleep at night, by all means. Confident it is," he retorts, and fuck do I love the way he plays back.

Not a stiff after all.

"Truce?" I extend my hand, waiting for him to relent and shake on it.

He glares at me with those midnight blue eyes, but for the first time since we've met, there's no hostility in them. It flirts the line of curiosity and challenge—two things I can work with.

He shakes my hand with earnest, electricity zinging through our palms as I feel his rough calluses scrape against my skin. He says nothing as he gets up from the table. All I'm left with is a smug grin and an incredible view of his body as he walks away in those fitted jeans and a Rays T-shirt, stretched perfectly across his broad back and shoulders.

His aura *drips* with sin.

And sin has never been so tempting.

4

WILLIAM

I Can Be Your Good Boy

Slipping the frayed, woven bracelet I wear for every game I start under my elbow sleeve, I sit back in my locker and get lost in the music blaring through my headphones.

Jimmy Eat World's "Sweetness" finishes playing just as Hughesy takes a seat at his locker beside me.

Slipping off my headphones, I nod at my new teammate. "Hughesy, did I hear you live on the beach?"

"Yeah, I live over on Sunset Cliffs, so not your traditional beach houses, but can't beat the views," he tells me as he works a muscle cream onto his strained left hamstring.

"Nice. I'm thinking about purchasing something oceanfront. Did you use a realtor?"

"Yeah, her name is Stefani. She's great. Let me know if you want me to send her contact information your way."

"That'd be awesome, man. Appreciate you." I slap Hughesy's back in thanks.

"Of course you'd live on the beach." Brooks scoffs, shaking his head so his shaggy black hair falls across his forehead.

"Aren't you supposed to play nice?" I retort with a quirked brow.

I've noticed he's not one to back down, so I'm not surprised when Brooks looks up at me with a shit-eating grin eclipsing his face. Leaning into my space, he murmurs, "You wanna play with me, Sin? With a name like that, I didn't think you'd like it nice. But if that's what does it for you, I can be your good boy."

His low, raspy tone has my stomach clenching involuntarily. And the way his warm breath scorches my neck has me wanting to crawl out of my skin. I flinch as if I've been burned.

The moment he pulls away, I shoot to my feet and head for the solo bathroom just outside the locker room. Needing a moment to collect myself, I shut and lock the door behind me. With my back to the door, I close my eyes and curse myself for letting him get under my skin again.

What is it about that cheeky attitude of his that has my chest heaving and my blood pumping?

He can be my good boy? There's nothing *good* about Brooks Warren. I have a feeling his version of "playing nice" is far different than Coach's.

It's no secret that he's into men, seeing as he's openly bisexual. I can't help but feel like he's toeing the line between giving me shit and . . . flirting? I don't know. Regardless, I don't like the way my body reacted to his voice and his breath on my skin.

Feeling a bout of nausea roll through me, I rush over to the toilet and empty the contents of my stomach the way I do before every game. No matter how many years I've played, and the hundreds of games I've started over the years, I throw up without fail each and every time.

As I'm rinsing out my mouth and splashing cool water on my face, there's a knock at the door.

I'm surprised to find Brooks there when I step out into the hallway.

He scratches his jaw and smirks at me, causing that damn dimple of his to pop. "I guess I thought the rumor around the league of the All-Star pitcher throwing up before every game was just that. What's the deal?"

My instincts say to shove my way past him, but the genuine curiosity sparkling in his eyes has me leaning against the wall and admitting, "Not sure. I've done it every game without fail since my first ever start."

His brows shoot up. "Shit, really? What about in high school and college?"

"Never."

"You're a weird one, Pretty Boy. Now step aside; I've gotta take a piss." He slaps me on the shoulder, and heat shoots down my arms from the contact.

"Someone should teach you some manners," I mutter under my breath, stepping back to put some much-needed space between us.

"You wanna teach me, *Daddy*?" he asks, leaning against the wall.

I sputter. "What the fuck did you just say?"

"I asked if you wanted to teach me some manners."

"Clearly. And then?" I question him with narrowed eyes.

"And then I called you daddy." He shrugs as if that isn't totally inappropriate to call another teammate. "You seem like the type of guy who likes women to call him Daddy. I bet you eat that shit up."

He needs to shut the fuck up and stop saying that word right now.

I clench my jaw in frustration before clearing my throat. "Can't say I've ever been referred to as *that* before this moment."

Rolling his bottom lip between his teeth, he shrugs in indifference. "Guess I was wrong about you. There's a first time for everything."

Yeah, like the first time I knock a teammate out before the start of the game. Shit, I'm feeling nauseous again.

Pushing past him, I rush back into the bathroom and slam the door shut behind me.

Brooks calls out from the other side of the door. "You've gotta get your shit together, man. Throwing up before every game doesn't fit right with the new nickname I've given you."

When he lets out a low chuckle, it's almost like he can see the middle finger I'm throwing his way right before I empty anything left in my stomach.

"The brunette with a navy Rays jersey on, three rows up from the left of the dugout. She's a total smoke show," I overhear Hughesy point out to Truett as I take a seat beside them on the bench between innings.

"Here," Brooks says as he throws my arm wrap to keep my shoulder warm while our team is at bat.

"Thanks," I mutter, grateful he reminded me because my new pitching coach is a stickler about recovery, and keeping my shoulder warm between innings is part of that.

"You're pitching one hell of a first game," Brooks tells me, and it's kind of hilarious the way his face pinches like it pains him to say it.

I huff out a laugh. "You look like you've got a stick shoved up your ass from paying me a small compliment."

Brooks sits back against the bench, manspreading in his catcher's gear as he folds his arms behind his head. "Trust me, that's not how I'd look if that were the case. But yeah, paying compliments to you is new for me."

"Hughesy, how are our prospects looking for tonight?" Brooks turns his head to ask him, looking like the picture of nonchalance.

Hughesy walks over and spits some seeds onto the floor of the dugout before he says, "I'm pretty sure the brunette I was just pointing out to Truett was the girl from the bar last week who said she'd be down to share before her friends were cockblocks and said they wanted to go to a different bar."

My brows crease. Share? As in share Hughesy with one of her friends?

Hughesy must read the question written on my face because he clarifies, "From time to time, Brooks and I like to share a girl if she's down."

Now I know my poker face is shit because my brows skyrocket to the brim of my ball cap.

Brooks bends over in laughter as does Hughesy before he says, "Oh don't look so scandalized, Sinclair. You'd think with a nickname like Sin you'd have gotten into a little threeway fun."

Brooks scoffs and fixes his gaze on me. "I'm almost certain Pretty Boy over here doesn't like sharing his toys, let alone his women."

"You make an awful lot of assumptions about me, and you seem oddly fixated on my sex life, Warren," I cut back.

Brooks arrogantly shrugs. "Not fixated. Just calling it like I see it."

"Well, you were wrong again. I can share my toys and my women, I just choose not to—share my toys, that is."

"Prove it."

"How?" I ask him, feathering my jaw in frustration.

"We've got an away game in Seattle next week and I happen to know a girl who is always down for a good time. Especially the threesome kind of fun. It's time to fuck around and find out, Sin."

"Consider it done, War. Text me the time and place." I regret the words the second they've left my mouth, especially when Brooks' eyes light up with mischief.

Rubbing his hands together, he looks me up and down and says, "Oh, this should be fun. I'll give my girl Deidre a call tonight."

5

BROOKS

Everything's Better in 3s

NOT EVEN A POST-WIN hot shower can ease the adrenaline thrumming through my blood.

I'm riding a fucking high after we've secured yet another win under our belt. And nothing gets me harder than winning. Especially on another team's home turf.

Well, that and a certain pretty boy pitcher who just happens to be the center of my thoughts lately—and my away game roomie thanks to Coach.

I can't tell if it's his polished exterior or the beast I know he's barely holding back—either way, it's got me fucked. He's insufferable, humorless, and exactly the kind of trouble I shouldn't want to get into.

But night after night, my fist knows better.

I've been strung out all week, ever since Sinclair hinted he might finally let me drag him into my favorite type of playtime—a night made for three.

I look down at my hardening length, deciding it's time to get out of the shower to hit up my own little pocket of sunshine in dreary-ass Seattle.

Toweling dry, I swipe my phone off the bathroom counter of my hotel room to type out a text.

Fuck yes.

Walking out into the room, a smile breaks on my face when I look at the tidiness of Will's bed compared to mine, his sheets neatly flat and pressed as if he never even slept in it.

The freak makes his bed every morning at the ass crack of dawn like housekeeping doesn't exist. Surely he grew up with maids and butlers who never let him lift a finger.

Maybe it's his pre-game ritual. I'm still getting to know my new teammate. He rarely comes out with us and usually retreats back to the room, passed out and snoring by the time I get back from being out with the boys.

I get that he's new to the team and was traded by his own father. I can't imagine the hit to the gut that must've been for him. But Sinclair is still a spoiled rich boy who's a neat freak and can't ever take a fucking joke.

So serious. So goddamn broody. Even his duffle bag sits neatly next to his perfectly made bed, whereas I look over at mine with clothes strewn across it and rumpled sheets.

No point in making it up now since Deidre will be here within the hour and the sheets are going to be on the floor when I'm done with her.

Hopefully when *we're* done with her.

God, I'm in dire need of a good fuck. My cock surges with the thoughts of her soft body so pliable in my hands. Then my mind shifts to a broad chest with rippling abs and taut muscles through-out.

He's firm and strong, piercing me with those midnight blue eyes and full lips I ache to bite and taste.

If Sinclair is a man of his word, then tonight should be no problem at all to dish out our depraved fantasies. My blood pulses straight between my legs, making it so I can't help but reach down and squeeze the head that's already leaking precum.

I need to know if he was just fucking around or if he's down for this. I'm flying on the adrenaline from the win tonight, and Sinclair can ride the wave with me or get the hell off.

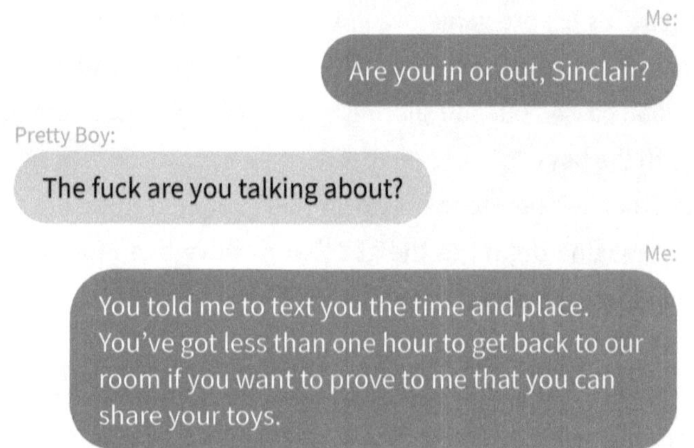

Three dots appear and disappear for what seems like forever. With my patience waning, I'm about to pull up Hughesy's text thread to sub in for the stiff until finally he responds—splitting a filthy smile on my face.

6

WILLIAM

Eyes On Me Pretty Boy

He said I had an hour, and I spent every fucking minute of it sec-ond-guessing whether or not I should do this. Anticipation heightens my senses to the point that I can hear them in the hallway before I've pressed my keycard against the lock to open it.

"Oh, fuck! I've missed you, baby," a feminine voice moans through the door, causing me to hesitate again.

If you cross the line, there's no going back.

"Isn't your teammate going to join us?" Brooks' little plaything asks.

Fuck it.

I practically slam the keycard against the lock, swinging the door open to find Brooks buck naked and tweaking the woman's nipples while she strokes his cock while wearing only a pink satin thong.

It's a sight I can't look away from, though I find myself questioning why instead of focusing on the way her dusty rose nipples harden beneath his touch, I'm fixated on the way her fist works up and down as she pumps his long, thick length.

And why, instead of focusing on the way she's positioned with her head nearly falling off the side of the mattress and thinking that'd be the perfect way for her to take me deep into her throat, I'm staring with hooded eyes at Brooks' ink that wraps around his torso, leading right to the smattering of hair just below his navel that leads to his impressive dick.

"He'll probably chicken out. He's all talk," Brooks tells her.

Instead of making myself known, I quietly shut the door behind me and toe off my shoes in the entryway of the room.

"Aw, that's too bad. You know how much I love when you share," she whines in a way that's actually kind of adorable instead of annoying.

"I'm sorry to disappoint, Warren," I drawl from the darkened entryway, stepping out of the shadows and shoving my hands in the pockets of my jeans. "This might be a foreign concept to you, but I'm a man of my word. I said I'd be here, and here I am."

"Yeah, well, you'll have to forgive me for assuming a guy with such a huge stick up his ass would actually participate in a threesome." I shrug off Brooks' remark. He's an ass, but I'm far too turned on and intrigued by the scene in front of me to turn back now.

It's not typical for me to drink in season, but I need something to take the edge off, so I make my way to the mini bar in the far corner of the hotel room and pour myself a glass of two whiskey shooters.

"I see you've started without me, but should we have Deidre sign an NDA?" I question.

Deidre snorts at that. "Already done. I know the drill," she assures me.

Instead of shooting back the whiskey, I take a seat on the chair in the corner of the room and sit back lazily, taking in the show before me.

Even with my gaze fixed on Deidre's luscious breasts, I can feel Brooks' eyes on me. It's only when he lets out a deep chuckle that I shift my gaze to his. He shakes his head at me and says, "That's the cuck chair."

Narrowing my eyes at him, I ask, "The what?"

"Come on, you have to have heard the term before. You're sitting in the cuck chair. Everyone knows the random arm chair in the corner of a hotel room is referred to as the cuck chair where someone sits to watch the significant other get off with another person," Brooks explains while Deidre continues pumping his length in her hand.

"Does that mean I get to call the shots? Or do most cucks remain quiet?"

"Oh, are you the domineering type of guy?" Deidre asks with excitement evident in her tone.

"Yeah. That alright with you, Princess?" I ask her.

Deidre bites her lip at my use of a pet name for her, but Brooks scoffs. "Princess? Guess that's fitting considering you're the Prince Charming of baseball."

"Shut up and climb onto the bed between her legs," I tell him gruffly, fed up with his theatrics.

I'm shocked when Brooks complies, rounding the bed before kneeling between Deidre's thighs. My stomach tightens as blood rushes straight to my cock. Who knew Brooks Warren could listen? Color me surprised as hell. The smirk he gives does something to me I can't decipher, or maybe it's that I don't want to.

"You just going to sit there and watch like a voyeur, Pretty Boy? Unless that's your thing. I can be down for that too," Brooks taunts, quirking a skeptical brow at me. The smug look on his face, combined with the way he reaches down and continues tweaking Deidre's nipple, has me gripping my thickening length over my jeans.

I'm hyper fixated on the way his large hands and deft fingers flick her nipples, and I find myself momentarily consumed with thoughts of his calloused fingers tracing a path over my own and down to my suddenly throbbing cock.

What the fuck? Where the hell did that mental image come from?

Needing to erase those thoughts, I shoot back my glass of whiskey and let out a huff as the liquor burns its way down my throat.

"Kiss me," Deidre murmurs to Brooks, reaching for his face.

I don't miss the way he hesitates to grant her request at first, shifting his eyes to me momentarily before leaning down and capturing her lips in a kiss that looks as sensual as it does possessive.

Their kiss turns heated, and I watch with rapt attention as Brooks grinds his hips against Deidre's. I squeeze my length hard through my jeans to find some relief, but it's no use. I'm too restrained and entirely too pent up to continue sitting back and watching.

"Eat her pussy, War." I rasp the command.

They break from their kiss, and the two of them look over at me with lustful eyes and playful smiles. Brooks shifts back and shoulders himself between Deidre's thighs. He places a delicate kiss over her thong before sliding the fabric to the side and licking a long stroke through her slit.

"So fucking good." The groan he lets out from her taste sends a bolt of lust straight through me.

Brooks circles her opening before thrusting two fingers inside her, causing Deidre's back to arch off the bed as she throws her head back in pleasure. When she turns her head and beckons me over to join them, it's all too much yet not nearly enough at the same time.

I set the glass down on the table and stand abruptly from my seat in the corner before pulling my shirt over my head and tossing it to the floor. Moving to the bedside where Deidre's head is lolled off the edge, I grip her chin and lift it so her gaze is fixed directly where I want her to focus her attention.

Deidre understands my unspoken request, reaching for my belt and unbuckling it before flicking open the button of my jeans. I push her hands aside as I finish stripping bare.

"Woah, big guy." Deidre looks down at Brooks. "We're going to have a lot of fun with this one."

When I chance a glance at him, I find Brooks' darkened gaze fixed on me. He manages to give me a devilish smirk, adding a wink for good measure, all while continuing to eat her out.

I find myself biting back my groan of approval, but it slips loose when Deidre roughly strokes my cock before guiding it to her lips.

She places a delicate kiss on the head of my dick before licking a path from the base of my shaft to the tip, where she swirls her tongue before taking me deep in her throat.

My hips thrust forward on instinct, causing her to inhale deeply through her nose so she can take more of me. The more Deidre works my cock, the more intensely Brooks eats her pussy, pumping his fingers in and out of her quicker and quicker, the sounds of her wetness filling the room until she moans around my length as her body convulses just before she squirts all over Brooks' face. He continues to suck her clit as she rides out her orgasm, but the sight of his cocky, self-assured smile when he sits back on his heels has me leaking precum down Deidre's throat.

Brooks reaches back to the bedside table where he's placed a box of condoms. He grabs one and sits back on his heels again as he rips it open with his teeth, spitting the sliver of foil and tossing the rest of the wrapper off to the side before rolling it over his thick length.

I'm far too entranced watching him work his thighs beneath Deidre's before lining himself up at her entrance.

"You ready for me, Princess?" he asks her, and my dick twitches in her mouth at his use of my nickname for her.

Deidre nods her head while her mouth remains wrapped around my length.

Brooks thrusts into her before throwing his head back and letting out a deep, guttural groan as if he's in ecstasy. If that's what he sounds like just entering her, what kinds of noises does he make when he comes? Fuck! Why do I care? What is happening to me?

I distract myself by kneading Deidre's breast in my palm—she's the perfect handful.

"Always so wet for me." Brooks' hands grip her hips so tightly he'll likely leave marks as he begins brutally pistoning his hips. The sound of skin slapping against skin echoes off the walls, met by our heavy breathing that harmonizes into a sinful melody between us. I'm not sure I've ever been this turned on in my life.

I roughly pinch Deidre's nipple between my fingers at the same time as Brooks uses his thumb to rub circles over her clit as if he's made it his mission to give her as many orgasms as humanly possible. Within moments, Deidre is pulling her mouth from my cock to let out a shrill cry as she comes for a second time.

Brooks' eyes trail me as I walk around the bed to his nightstand and grab a condom from the pack. I'm quick to roll it onto my length before setting a knee on the bed, but I freeze, hesitating with my decision to be this close to a naked Brooks as he continues to thrust in and out of her pussy. He smells like sex and transgressions, and I have to hold myself back from breathing him deeper into my lungs.

"Step aside. My turn," I grind out, sounding far more hostile than I should in this moment of shared pleasure. But I can't help it; I'm frustrated as hell at these confusing feelings of lust building inside of me.

Brooks pulls out of her, and his shoulder brushes mine as he stands from the bed. I do my best to ignore the goosebumps that rise in the wake of his accidental touch, but I can't stop my body's reaction to it. I curse beneath my breath as I trade places with Brooks.

He sheds himself of his condom, tossing it on my nightstand, and I narrow my eyes at it in disgust. By now he knows I prefer things clean and tidy, and it's as if he makes it his mission to dirty things up at my expense.

Brooks looks at me, waggling his eyebrows and bringing his bottom lip between his teeth as his cheeks curve up into a devious smirk.

"On your hands and knees," I say gruffly to Deidre.

She does as I told her to, facing Brooks while arching her back to give me the perfect view of her round ass and dripping pussy.

Deidre reaches for his length, roughly stroking it before bringing it to her mouth. I scoot closer to her before lining myself up and pushing inside her, slowly giving her inch by inch as I pull out and press my hips forward until she finally takes nearly all of me. She wasn't wrong—I'm well endowed, but she manages to take more of my eight inches than most women have.

I grip her hip with one hand and slap her creamy ass with the other. "You were right. Her pussy is so good, so wet, but you didn't mention how tight she is." Making eye contact with Brooks, my cock throbs inside her pussy. "You're squeezing me so tight," I tell her through gritted teeth.

She pulls off Brooks' dick with a pop and begs, "More! Please!"

Finding my rhythm, I grip her hips with both hands and give her exactly that.

My eyes roll to the back of my head as I continue to pound into Deidre's pussy, but when I suddenly find myself wishing it was Brooks' fist I was thrusting into, I hesitate. Shooting my eyes open wide to banish those thoughts, I'm met with Brooks' fiery eyes on me.

Without breaking eye contact, he grabs the back of Deidre's head and begins pistoning his hips faster.

I find myself matching his punishing rate when he says, "You gonna come in her tight pussy while I come down her throat, Sin? Let's make her collateral damage for when Sin meets War."

Looking down at her pussy, I squeeze my eyes shut and try to focus on the fact that it's Deidre I'm fucking and push the fantasy of it being Brooks to the far recesses of my mind never to think of again. But it's impossible when Brooks growls, "No. Eyes on me when you come, Pretty Boy."

My gaze shoots to his, and those lustful, forbidden fantasies of me fucking Brooks, not Deidre, consume me as his blazing gaze stays focused on me. Need fills me as pleasure courses through my blood, and I can feel my impending orgasm.

When he nods at me, it's as if he can read my mind, somehow knowing I'm thinking of him. And when he bites his plush bottom lip and tilts his chin back to expose his Adam's apple, all while keeping eye contact, I thrust once, twice, three times before I'm coming with an intensity I've never felt before.

What in the actual fuck was that? And why do I find myself wishing for it to happen again sooner rather than later?

WILLIAM

WAR STORIES

MY THUMB CONTINUES TO tap anxiously against my steering wheel as I question what I'm doing right now.

Wondering why the fuck I'm sitting in my SUV with my engine idling at the curb outside Brooks Warren's parents' house. Something is seriously wrong with me. Throwing my head back against my headrest, I look up at the sky through my sunroof and squint in search of something—for what, I'm not sure. Maybe to see if the sky is falling? Surely, something apocalyptic has to be happening to make sense of why Brooks asked me after practice today if I wanted to join him for dinner at his parents' house. The no was on the tip of my tongue until he added I'd be an idiot to turn down one of his mom's home-cooked meals and that he'd take it as a personal slight if I declined his invitation.

We'd been making progress toward tolerating one another on and off the field—well, until the other night that is, but I refuse to go there. Point is, prior to *that*, we'd had something akin to camaraderie.

I shouldn't be here. This isn't a good idea—not when it was only two nights ago that I came the hardest I've ever come in my life all while staring directly into Warren's eyes.

"Goddamn it!" I shout, hitting the steering wheel in frustration.

My chest heaves as I smooth my hand through my hair, my best attempt at taming the piece that had strayed onto my forehead. A knock on my passenger window startles me out of my spiral. I scowl when I realize it's Brooks who interrupted my moment of self-loathing.

Pressing the button to roll down the window, I hiss, "What do you want?"

Brooks rests his forearms on the door and leans in with a cocksure smirk that irritates me far more than it should. "Figures a pretty boy like you would drive a black Range Rover. This is my extremely shocked face," he deadpans.

Narrowing my eyes on him, I grumble, "Ah, and here I was under the impression you had a modicum of decorum. But I guess I was wrong if this is how you treat your guests."

"Pretty sure you weren't complaining about my lack of manners the other night," he mocks, and there it is. Leave it to him to bring *that* up within the first sixty seconds of me being here.

"For fuck's sake," I growl, facing forward and struggling to take a deep breath so I don't reach over and strangle him. Although, maybe I should so I could wipe the smug look off his face.

"Ease up, *William*, I'm just giving you shit," he says, and the way he calls me by my full name has my stomach tightening. "Come on, my mom's famous moussaka is waiting for us."

At the mention of food, my stomach clenches for an entirely different reason. Fuck, I'm not even sure the last time I had a home-cooked meal. Growing up, we always had a live-in chef. My mother used to say cooking was beneath her. That way of life stuck with me when I got my own place. I hired a nutritionist to cook and prep my meals in St. Louis, but since moving to San Diego, I haven't found a new one yet.

I get out and click the lock on my keys as I round the front end, causing Brooks to scoff. "Worried someone's gonna steal your precious? Maybe you should double check you locked it."

It's only then I take in what Brooks is wearing and feel what I hope to God isn't a blush heating my cheeks. He's got on a flannel-patterned shirt that's unbuttoned with a white T-shirt underneath. The sleeves of his white and green flannel are rolled up, displaying his corded and tatted forearms. The black watch I've noticed he never removes aside from games is adorned on his left wrist while his other hand is tucked into the pair of black, distressed jeans that, on anyone else, would fit relaxed, but instead cling to his muscular thighs. And in place of the black Vans I've grown accustomed to seeing him in, he's wearing a pair of dark brown boots. He looks . . . My eyes snap up to his when I realize I was just detailing what he was wearing, and the smug expression I'm met with has me gritting my teeth.

Shit.

I veer my gaze down the street, doing my best to avoid eye contact. His parents live about twenty minutes inland from my rental. Their home is modest and nicely kept, clearly taken care of, which can't be said for some of the other houses down the street. My eyes catch on the squeaky clean, white SUV in his parents' driveway.

Nodding toward his Audi, I quirk a brow. "I'm not too concerned considering your vehicle is just as likely to be stolen as mine."

Brooks looks over his shoulder and then shakes his head. "Not mine. My mom's," he corrects, and I must do a poor job of hiding my surprise. He runs his hand down his jaw and shrugs. "They did a lot for me and my little sis growing up. Made a lot of sacrifices and worked way too many hours of overtime so I could live out my dream. It was the least I could do."

"I see," I hum in response, unsure of what else to say.

Brooks nods once before taking me in and shaking his head at me. "Thought I told you to dress casual?"

I look down at my navy button down and light gray chinos with my crisp, white sneakers. Focusing back on him, I say, "This is casual."

"You're wearing a collared dress shirt," he points out, as if that means anything.

"But it's untucked and I didn't wear a dress belt or tie." I pause to give him a look that says *Fuck off, thank you very much*. "This is about as casual as it gets in my wardrobe."

Brooks lifts his hands in surrender. "My bad. Should've figured a stiff like you would dress like you're going to the yacht club when I told you casual."

With his completely insincere apology hanging between us, he turns toward the front door of his parents' house.

"What did you say your mom made for dinner?" I ask as we walk up the front steps.

"Moussaka. It's the Greek version of lasagna only a fuck ton better because *i mamá mou* made it," he explains.

Wait a minute. "Did you just speak Greek?" I question incredulously.

"*Naí*," he replies, which I'm pretty certain means yes.

Hold on. How did I not know he was Greek, or at least part Greek? And why the hell am I staring at him with a dumbfounded expression on my face?

Before I can think any further on that, the front door swings open to reveal who I can only assume is Brooks' mother. She's a strikingly beautiful woman, petite in height and stature, with vibrant emerald eyes that mirror her son's, and short, raven hair with salt and pepper mixed in.

"Welcome!" his mother greets us, pulling me into a hug before I can even get a grasp on what's happening.

"*Mamá*," Brooks scolds lightheartedly, chuckling at his mother's antics. "Boundaries." He chortles out the word, which his mother completely disregards.

"Let me get a look at you," she says, stepping back and eyeing me from head to toe. "When my son told us William Sinclair was joining us for dinner, I thought my husband was going to pass out."

Out of the corner of my eye, I see Brooks roll his, and I decide it's time to turn on my irresistible Sinclair charm, if for nothing other than to mess with him.

"Thank you for having me for dinner, Mrs. Warren. It's a pleasure to meet you."

"Oh, gosh, none of that 'Mrs. Warren' nonsense. Elena. Call me Elena."

"That's a beautiful name," I tell her as she brings me in for another hug and thanks me while I peer at her son over her shoulder, shooting him a wink. Brooks narrows his eyes at me and flips me the bird just as his mom turns around, though she unfortunately misses his obscene gesture.

"Please, come in, come in," Elena says, waving us inside their ranch-style home.

The interior looks like it's been recently renovated with dark hardwood floors throughout the open-concept living area the entryway leads into. The mixture of the wood and stone materials in combination with the white-washed walls give it a coastal feel, and the decor further emphasizes the aesthetic.

Elena gestures for us to follow her into the kitchen, where she pulls out a barstool for me to sit in.

I murmur my thanks then tell her, "I like your vehicle out front. My mother drives the same model Audi, even the same color."

"Oh, that old thing?" she questions jokingly, gesturing toward the driveway and shaking her head. "Thank you, my sweet boy purchased it for me. I swear, I've never been more upset to receive a gift than I was the day he gave it to me—big red bow and all. I begged him to take it back and told him it's far too extravagant, especially considering he'd already paid off our mortgage for us." She turns to Brooks and cups his cheeks. "But that's just the way my Brooksy is. A mama's boy through and through, no matter how old he gets."

"Brooksy?" I echo, fighting back a snort.

Brooks' cheeks heat ever so slightly, but he smiles down lovingly at his mom instead of feeding into my badgering. A pang of jealousy hits me as I watch the two of them interact, knowing my relationship with my own mother couldn't be farther from what appears to be their tight-knit bond.

"Don't coddle the boy, Lena," a deep voice booms from the other side of the house before a tall, barrel-chested man walks out of what appears to be a bedroom off of the dining room.

His head is down, focused on something in his hands—a shirt maybe? When he lifts his head and his gaze lands on me, he murmurs "Holy shit" at the same time as I think it because in his hands is my rookie jersey from the Philly. I don't even need to see the front of it to know their old logo is on it because it's the original burgundy the franchise retired during my second season.

"Well I'll be damned. Brooks told me you were joining us for dinner, but I'd convinced myself he was playing another one of his pranks on me. Pinch me, Son," his father says, completely awestruck as he holds up his arm for Brooks to do just that.

"Jesus, are you for real?" Brooks questions, shaking his head in disbelief.

"Serious as a heart attack," his dad replies.

"That's not fuckin' funny considering you're only a year out from having just had one yourself," Brooks scolds.

His dad smacks him on the shoulder. "Lighten up, would ya? It's not every day *the* William Sinclair comes to dinner." Walking over to me, he holds out his hand for me to shake. "It's a pleasure to meet you, kid. My name's Hank, and I see you've already met my beautiful bride. We're glad you could join us."

"Thank you for having me, Mr. Warren."

"Call me Hank. I insist."

"Alright, Hank. I appreciate you welcoming me into your home. It's been far too long since I've had a home-cooked meal," I admit somewhat bashfully.

"It's our pleasure," Hank says before lifting the jersey in his hands. "There's just one caveat: you don't get dinner unless I get this rookie jersey of yours signed."

"Dad! Stop fangirling. You're embarrassing not only me but yourself," Brooks huffs in exasperation.

Elena chooses that moment to chime in. "Don't act as if you aren't guilty of fangirling yourself, my boy. As I recall, you called me after your first pitching practice together a few weeks ago and talked my ear off, going on and on about how talented Will is."

"Mom," Brooks chastizes, his cheeks heating crimson.

Interesting. So maybe it turns out he didn't hate me as much as he led on.

"Not to mention the giant poster you had on your wall of him when you were in high school," Hank adds.

"Dad, are you fucking serious?" Brooks grumbles, looking equal parts annoyed and mortified.

At this point, I'm grinning like the cat that ate the canary. I will most definitely be circling back to that little factoid at a later date, but before I can give him any shit, the front door opens and in walks a girl with sleek, raven hair down to her waist. As she gets closer, I realize she isn't a girl, but a very petite woman who appears to be in her early twenties. Going by her sage green eyes, I assume she must be Brooks' little sister he's warned a few of the guys not to entangle themselves with.

"Ah, Jade, there you are," Elena says, wrapping her in a warm hug.

"Fashionably late as usual," Brooks teases, to which his sister holds up her middle finger in reply behind her mother's back.

"Oh fuck off, golden child," Jade retorts with a playful lilt.

"Language," Elena scolds.

Jade steps out of her mother's embrace and apologizes. "I'm sorry, *Mamá*."

"It's alright. I'm just glad you made it home finally. It's been too long," Elena says, brushing a strand of Jade's long hair behind her ear. "I've missed you, *agápi mou*."

She offers her mother a soft smile. "I'm here now, and that's all that matters."

Suddenly, Elena's expression hardens and her shoulders stiffen. "What in heaven's name is on your nose?"

Jade smirks. "You like it? I got my nose pierced while at school with Quinn."

"Jade, no! Tell me this can be taken out immediately. Why would you do this to your beautiful face?" Elena admonishes.

"Oh, come on. It's not that big of a deal."

"It is! You're about to get a full-time job. You can't very well interview with that metal in your nose like that."

A mischievous smile lights up Jade's face. "Relax, *Mamá*. It's fake."

"Fake? Oh, thank heavens."

Jade takes a deep breath and sighs in content. "Is that moussaka I smell?"

"I made your favorite," Elena tells her, turning back to the kitchen and putting on a pair of oven mitts. "Though now I'm questioning if I should've, considering your prank about the fake piercing."

"I'd never do that to you, *Mamá*," Brooks coos innocently, adding fuel to the fire.

With their mom's back to them, Jade elbows Brooks in the ribs and murmurs, "Would it kill you to be on my side for once in your life?"

"Ouch, you little shit," Brooks grumbles, rubbing his side. "What kinda brother would I be if I didn't give you a little shit from time to time?"

"This girl is the cause of all my gray hairs, I swear." Then, Elena turns to me. "Do you have any sisters or siblings, Will?"

I falter, a knot forming in my stomach from her question. "Yes, two, a brother and a sister."

"Well, I hope she's a lot nicer to you and your mom than this one is to me," Elena teases, pointing to Jade while completely unaware of the fissure down my chest her lighthearted words cause.

"Brooks, would you and Will set the table, please?" she asks, and Brooks being the mama's boy he is, dutifully grabs plates and forks before nodding to a cabinet and asking if I'll grab some glasses.

I follow him over to the dining room and trail behind him with the glasses, placing one in front and to the right of each plate he sets down.

Pausing, I look over to find Brooks staring at me strangely.

"Are you good?" he asks.

Furrowing my brows in confusion, I assure him, "Of course. Why wouldn't I be?"

Brooks shrugs. "I don't know. You just seem like you're in your own head. But what I do know is my family can be a lot to take in. We're not everyone's cup of tea, but you're being a good sport about it."

Giving him a polite smile and a curt nod, I pray he'll change the topic. Only he doesn't have to because in storms Jade with serving utensils in hand. She hip checks Brooks out of the way, and he feigns being hurt.

The simple sibling exchange makes me miss Abigail and her feisty personality—makes me long for the carefree days we'd banter and play together before everything changed.

Before I can get too far in my head, Brooks pulls out his phone and shoots me a shit-eating grin.

"What's that look for?" I ask.

He shakes his head and then looks up while pocketing his phone. "If you'd check the team group chat, you'd see the guys wanna go out tonight. Ever been to a club, Sinclair?"

8
BROOKS

I Kissed A Girl But I Wish It Was Him

IF I HAD TO bet on a place where William "The Stiff" Sinclair swore he'd never be, I'd put my money on a nightclub. Too many people, too much noise, and way too much danger for his spotless reputation.

Yet here we are.

I still can't believe I convinced him to come out tonight. Our dinner earlier was . . . nice. I don't know if it was my mom's moussaka that softened my heart toward Will, or the googly eyes my dad was making at him all evening. Either way, I find myself more eager by the day to peel back the layers guarding this enigma of a man.

Why am I so invested in learning more about him? He's kind of fuckin' mean, but that's nothing new to me. I get I'm a bit of a brat. I haven't exactly made his transfer easy. But the more I get to know him, the more he surprises me.

My family seemed to love him, and he was polite enough to appease my mother and sister, which isn't always easy. Dad was a little star-struck, so I guess that worked in my favor. Will ate everything with a smile and even offered to wash the dishes.

But I could tell something about him was off as the evening went on. Maybe a night out can shake him out of whatever weirdness was clouding over him. The fact that I care this much throws me for a loop, but it's nothing a shot of tequila or two can't fix.

As we head toward the VIP section where our teammates wait, my eyes betray me. I steal a glance at the way his chinos hug the firmness of his ass. I smirk at his attempt at "casual." Not that I'm complaining about the way his collared shirt clings to those sculpted muscles.

My thoughts instantly drift to the other night, when I got to see those muscles bare and slick with sweat. Every powerful thrust of his hips has been on replay in my head since. The way his eyes locked onto mine as we came together.

Fuck. Now my dick is straining against my jeans just thinking about it.

"There he is!" Truett shouts from behind the velvet rope.

I grip Will's shoulder, guiding him forward. "You ready for a fun night, Sinclair?"

"Don't make me regret it."

I chuckle, nodding my head to the bouncer who lets us past the rope. "You should know by now that a night with me is anything but regretful."

Will just shakes his head, following a step behind me as Truett and Hughesy appear, shots already in hand.

"Bottoms up, boys," Hughesy grins, pressing a glass of clear liquid into each of our hands.

"I'll pass," Will mutters.

My immediate reaction is to give him shit. Truett and Hughesy are persistent, wanting to see our star pitcher let loose a bit. Sinclair, being ever so stoic, politely pushes away his shot. To my surprise, he's actually being a good sport while my two best friends drunkenly poke and prod at him.

I step between them and Will, taking his neglected shot for myself. "Alright, alright. That's enough boys. The Stiff here said he's good." I throw back both shots without a flinch, relishing the burn as it travels down my throat.

Out of the corner of my eye, I catch Will staring at my mouth. I drag my tongue slowly across my lips just to fuck with him.

Is it just me, or is Sinclair blushing?

He quickly looks away, shoving his hands deep into the front pockets of his chinos. Truett and Hughesy have already lost interest, slipping past the velvet rope in search of a couple cleat chasers.

I lean in, my breath brushing his ear. "Getting shy on me now, Sin?"

"Don't start." He pins me with a hard stare—but if I didn't know any better, I'd swear it's nothing but liquid heat.

I toss my hands up in mock surrender, a dark chuckle rumbling from my chest. "*Relax.* I'm just saying, you don't have to hide from me."

Will puts some space between us, clearing his throat. "I'm not hiding. This just isn't my scene. I'm too old for this shit."

Slinging my arm around his shoulder, I steer us toward the VIP bar. If I can get a little liquid courage in him, maybe he'll loosen up and have some fun. Something tells me indulgence isn't Will's strong suit.

That night between us could've been a fluke—a really fucking hot fluke—but a fluke nonetheless. But now, he's in my head, under my skin, burning me from the inside out.

"You act like you're fuckin' ninety years old. Have a drink; get to know the guys. You're one of us now, whether you wanna believe it or not. That means something."

Will releases a long breath, stretching his hands behind his head. Part of his shirt rides up, revealing that smattering of dark hair I'd love nothing more than to run my hands over. But I need to reel it in. Just because we had one insanely hot night together doesn't mean he'd want to do it again, no matter how badly I'm dying for a repeat.

"Alright. One drink, War."

Her body melts against mine as I grip her hips, guiding her into the slow grind of the music. The sweet scent of her perfume lingers in the air, pulling me in as I bury my face in the curve of her neck. Her arms slip around my shoulders, locking me closer, and together we move as one with every heavy thump of the bass.

I'm right in the sweet spot of not too far gone, but just loose enough that I'm not seeing double. Every sense is heightened, and I'm loving the way this girl feels in my hands.

But it isn't her soft skin or tempting curves that send goosebumps racing across my body. It's a pair of midnight-blue eyes holding me hostage from across the dance floor. Eyes with so much mystery it makes my head fucking spin. And there he is—taunting me.

I don't know what game Will's playing tonight. After I bought him that one drink, he's dodged me at every turn. Yeah, I told him to get to know the guys, but I didn't expect him to flat-out ignore me.

The way he's watching me right now only fuels me, though. I think the girl I'm dancing with is named Belinda. Or Linda. Maybe Lisa? Whatever. She's the perfect distraction from the storm Sinclair stirs in my head.

I sink into the rhythm with her, our bodies moving in sync, but my gaze never strays from his.

Hmm . . . what would happen if I just . . .

With a slow drag of my fingers, I sweep blondie's hair aside, softly kissing her neck. I watch those midnight eyes darken, and the tight clench of his jaw only sends me further into this hypnotic tether between us. I grip her chin and claim her lips—yet my stare never wavers.

I deepen the kiss, swallowing her moan when I'm suddenly yanked back by the collar of my shirt.

"That's my fucking girl you're touching, asshole!" a waspy-looking guy with an uppity sneer shouts in my face.

He cocks his fist, ready to swing. I brace for the hit when Sinclair comes out of nowhere, slamming the guy to the ground.

They grapple in a blur of fists and grunts, until the guy manages to scramble on top of Will.

Belinda-Linda-Lisa screeches for her boyfriend to let go, but not before he lands a clean shot to Will's mouth. I lunge for him, fingers snagging his shirt, when security barrels in to break it up.

My stomach plummets at the sight of Will's split lip, blood trickling down his chin. Security tries to grab him, but I shove them back, cupping his face to check for more damage.

"Fuck, Will—are you okay? You're bleeding."

His eyes are wild, chest heaving, clothes rumpled from the fight. But when his gaze locks onto mine, my pulse spikes. A dark, consuming possession oozes out of him, crackling the air between us.

For a moment, time stops. My thumbs sweep gently over his cheeks, but then the spell shatters as the crowd closes in, cell phone lights flashing like stars.

Shit.

Will jolts out of it, shoving me back. "Get off of me," he mutters, before storming through the sea of onlookers.

I chase after him, ignoring my teammates calling out behind me. "Will! Stop!"

He doesn't even look back, storming toward the exit. "Sinclair! Why are you being an asshole? I was just trying to help."

He shoves through the door, and I follow, the heavy summer air clinging to my sweat-slick skin.

"Just leave me alone, War," he throws over his shoulder, stomping down the alley.

He's halfway down when all the blood rushes to my head, frustration coursing through my veins. Why the fuck did he hit that guy? Was it for me? I need to know. I say the only thing I know that can make him listen.

"You know I didn't take you for a chicken-shit, Sinclair."

He stops. "What the hell are you talking about?"

I stand at the end of the alley, slowly stalking toward him. "Was that you trying to defend my honor? Is that why you hit that asshole? For me?" I goad, a smirk curling my lips.

"Honor?" He scoffs. "You call sticking your tongue down the throat of a taken woman honor?"

Well, I didn't know she was taken. Maybe I let my selfish little game go too far. A wave of guilt ripples through me when I see his mouth starting to swell.

"Then why interfere? Why not let that asshole pummel me if you thought I deserved it?"

We're a breath apart now, toe-to-toe. The blood from his lip is fresh, shining under a street light. It makes him more beautiful than before, a little disheveled and rough around the edges. Far from his clean-cut persona. It makes me *fucking hard.*

"We're teammates. I would've stepped in for any of you."

A sarcastic laugh escapes me. "There you go lying again. You can lie to yourself all you want, but you're not fooling me." I swallow hard, pressing my chest against his. "The way you were watching me made it pretty fucking obvious."

"And what's that?" Will grits out, jaw tight and fists clenched.

"That you want me."

9

WILLIAM

Whatever Helps You Sleep At Night

With my chest heaving against his, I freeze on the spot. "What the fuck did you just say to me?"

"You heard me."

"No, I don't think I did. Because if you said what I think you just said, we've got a problem."

He nods his head once. "Believe me, we've got plenty of problems. Your denial being at the forefront of them."

"I don't want you," I grit out, clenching my jaw.

"Say it again. Maybe I'll believe the lie this time."

"I don't. Fucking. Want you."

Brooks lets out a low chuckle. "See, here's the thing. I might believe that had I not caught on to the way you look at me—the way you've been watching me for weeks now." He pauses, his chest heaving against mine. "You wanna know *why* I know that? Because I've been watching you too. Obsessively. You're constantly on my radar—my newest compulsion, my sole fixation. And when I'm not physically around you, I can't get you outta my fuckin' head," Brooks rasps, pounding his finger against his temple.

He somehow manages to step impossibly closer, moving to murmur in my ear. "The other night—the one you're so keen on forgetting—plays like a reel over and over again in my mind. Just thinking about it gets my dick hard. But it has nothing to do with sharing. Nothing to do with the woman who was between us. I'm sure I don't have to spell it out for you, but because you're in such denial, I will . . . the moment your eyes connected with mine while I watched you fall apart, I realized my attraction to you was mutual."

Brooks pulls back just barely, only enough to stare at my lips. Unable to fight this pull, my gaze drops to his lips too, and when he realizes, he hisses in approval.

The way his chest heaves against mine, causing the fabric of our shirts to rub together, has my control hanging by a thread. I grip his shirt and shove him away only to pull him right back in.

"Sure feels like you want me, Sin." To make his point, he presses his hips against mine, and it's only then I realize what he's referring to. My length throbs achingly between us, making the truth in his statement apparent.

"You're bleeding," he points out, cupping my face in his hands. Brooks parts my mouth and swipes his calloused thumb across my swollen, bloodied bottom lip.

"Thanks for stating the obvious," I murmur, all of sudden feeling breathless.

"I must be rubbing off on you; you almost sounded like me for a second," he tosses back.

With his eyes locked on mine, he licks his lips, and something about that small gesture has me throwing my inhibitions to the wind.

"Shut up," I tell him in a deep-chested growl, pulling him to me and slamming our lips together.

In a battle for dominance, our lips open and our tongues move together in perfect synchrony. Brooks whimpers at the first swipe of his tongue, though I can't be sure if it's from the taste of my blood or what we're doing, which is full-on making out.

He grabs my hair and tugs tightly, causing me to groan against his lips as he grinds his hips against mine. His belt buckle presses into my lower stomach, and that in combination with his hard length rubbing against my own thickening cock has me spiraling.

I find myself wondering what it'd be like to unbuckle his belt and slip my hand beneath the waistband of his jeans. He's so hard, so fucking ready for me.

A noise from across the alleyway breaks the spell he was putting me under, and I push him away, my chest heaving as I struggle to say, "I'm not fucking gay."

With my fingers still fisted in his shirt, it's as if I can't push him away, my hands refusing to let him go.

Brooks shrugs; he'd look unaffected if it wasn't for his heavy breathing filling the alleyway. "So? Me neither."

I narrow my eyes at him. "Well, you've been with men before, and that's just not me. I'm straight."

Brooks shakes his head and lets out a low, maniacal chuckle. "Yeah, keep telling yourself that, Pretty Boy. Whatever helps you sleep at night."

10

BROOKS

Moony Eyes

I'M GETTING GOOD AT memorizing the back of Will's head. Sunlight cuts through the bus window, gilding the tan on his thick neck and catching on the silver chain resting there. Blond strands slip from beneath his hat, and I ache to tug them just to feel them against my fingers again.

I know exactly what those blond strands feel like between my fingers. So soft, just like those lips. God, I want to pull those noises out of him again from when our mouths fused together. Memories of the groans and deep-chested growls send a shiver down my neck, all the way to my toes.

It ended way too fast, with him leaving me there in that dark alley breathless and painfully hard.

I'm not fucking gay.

The memory of his words burn as I stare at the back of his infuriatingly beautiful head. Three days of silence. Even at practice he kept his distance, every ounce of focus funneled into his pitches. Great for the team. Brutal for my heart.

A painful jab nails me in the ribs. "Ow, fucker! What the hell was that for?"

"What's with the moony eyes at Sinclair?" Truett grins, eyes sparkling.

"I don't have moony eyes."

Truett leans back in his seat, lacing his fingers behind his head with a playful smirk. "Oh yes, you do. You look exactly like this." He bats his lashes in an exaggerated flutter, glazing his eyes over and puckering his lips into ridiculously kissy faces.

"Fuck off, Ham," I say, fighting back a smile.

"Didn't think Golden Boy swung that way."

Before I can answer, the bus jerks to a stop in front of our hotel. I stand, stretching my arms overhead, careful to avoid Truett's searching stare.

The thing is, that kiss has me reeling. How could something feel so right, yet throw me into a death spiral all at once? With Will's silence, I can only assume he's probably feeling the same way.

I knew of my sexuality from a young age. It was simple, really. I liked girls just as much as I liked boys. There were assholes growing up who would make fun of me, calling me every slur in the book. But I was one of the lucky ones who had a support system. Two loving parents who accepted me with no questions asked, and a little sister who'd lay out anyone who would look at me wrong.

"War? You just gonna ignore me?" Truett teases, rising from his seat.

I watch Will hustle down the steps of the bus, and I shove past my teammates to catch up to him. I'm over the silent treatment. Patience only goes so far when it comes to unraveling the puzzle that is William Sinclair. I need him to quit hiding and be straight with me. We kissed—so fucking what? If he wants to pretend there's nothing between us, then he can damn well say it to my face.

My feet hit the asphalt, and I spot him yanking his duffel from beneath the bus.

"Sinclair!" I call out.

He looks up, our eyes locking, tension sparking in the space between us. My body moves toward him before I even register the thought. His mouth parts, like he's finally about to speak.

"William!" a deep voice booms, cutting through the moment.

By the hotel entrance stands a tall man in a sleek gray suit, a woman nearly his height clinging to his arm. It doesn't take a genius to figure out who they are. The man's scowl is a mirror of the one Will throws me on the daily. And the woman who has a matching set of midnight blue eyes stares at Will with unshed tears as she clutches tighter to the man's arm.

Will's body visibly tenses, his fists gripping the strap of his duffel so tight his knuckles blanch. I watch as he takes a deep breath, head hung low like he's psyching himself up. I'm already walking toward him, pulled by an urgent need to comfort him.

Just as I'm about to reach out to him, he takes a few reluctant strides toward the couple, stopping in front of them without a flicker of affection.

I'm just close enough to hear a heated exchange, but too far to make out any specific words. Media press and league gossip don't compare to seeing the elusive owner of the St. Louis Bullfrogs. Jameson Sinclair exudes power, even just in his stance.

But the way Will avoids his father's gaze, hands on his hips like he's ready to dip out of whatever the hell they're talking about, says volumes. Even I'm shocked at myself for the protective feelings surging through me. The entire exchange has me on edge, my nerves spiking when his father leans in, face tight with barely contained anger.

The whole sight is jarring. Will's not what you call an open book. It's like pulling teeth to get that man to open up. Even at dinner with my family, he kept those walls high, hiding behind that perfect golden-boy mask. I can't help the small ache forming in the center of my chest when Will stomps off past his parents and through the automatic doors of the hotel.

Truett sidles up beside me, hefting my duffel onto my shoulder. "Told you. Moony eyes." He laughs, snatching the cap off my head and ruffling my hair as he strolls past.

A smack on my ass jolts me out of my daze. "You coming, *papi?*" Mateo calls over his shoulder with a smirk, jerking his chin for me to follow.

Clearing my throat, physically here but all my thoughts fixed on Will, I reply, "Right behind you."

The upside of being Will's roommate is there will be no way he can avoid me anymore. His vow of silence ends now.

Despondent and distant, Will doesn't notice when I enter our room as he gazes out of the large window. He's hiding those large hands in his pockets, tension buzzing off of him like a current. He doesn't turn until the door clicks shut behind me.

His lips twist into a frown, but I refuse to let it drag down the mood he's set since I walked in.

"Whoa, relax, Sinclair. I know you're thrilled to see me—just take it easy," I tease, hands raised in mock surrender.

Nothing. Not even a hint of a smile.

"I'm not in the mood, Brooks."

"Ah, Brooks now is it? Well, I gave you three days to sulk. Time's up. We're talking."

He turns back toward the window, voice flat. "There's not much to say."

Sharp words press against my tongue, but then I remember the way Will's face looked as his father leaned into him with disappointment etched in his face. How his shoulders locked tight with the weight of that exchange.

His parents showing up might not be the only reason he's been avoiding me, but it's sure as hell why he's clinging so hard to this silent treatment. He lets out a slow exhale, his face tilting up toward the ceiling.

"What do you want me to say, Brooks?"

"The truth," I quickly reply. "But I realize you might not be ready for that yet."

His eyes snap to me at that. So it seems I've struck a nerve. Good.

"We've got a game to get ready for. Look—" He lets out a heavy breath. "I'm fine. Just let me get my head on straight, alright?"

I shrug my shoulders, saying nothing as I place my duffel down on my bed. I don't really have anything in particular I'm looking for as I shuffle around inside my bag, the heat of Will's gaze on me pricking my skin.

He moves in my periphery, but my eyes stay downcast on the contents of my bag.

The mattress dips, and I glance up to find Will sitting on the edge of my bed, elbows braced on his knees, chin resting against his fists as he stares at me. My heart picks up speed, thumping hard in my chest.

"I'm sorry," Will whispers, so soft I almost miss it. "I've been an asshole to you."

Drawing a steady breath, I shove my bag aside and sit beside him. The apology was unexpected. Something about Will lowering his walls and showing me just a sliver of vulnerability has me aching for more.

I hold my tongue, fucking terrified that if I say the wrong thing, he'll clam up and shut me out again. As much as I hate to admit it, Will Sinclair has me in a goddamn chokehold. One look from the man, and I'm undone—shaken and thrilled all at once.

"I wanted to talk to you so many times . . . I just . . ." He scrubs both palms over his face. "You make me crazy."

Our thighs press together, the warmth from our bodies emanating off our skin. I make him crazy? Crazy good, crazy bad? The questions rush through me so fast it makes my head spin. Will bobs his knee up and down like a nervous tic, and I don't know—something about that makes my lips turn up in the smallest of smiles.

I make him crazy. I make him nervous. I make him *feel* something.

Taking a risk, I slowly reach for his hand and lace our fingers together. He stiffens for a split second, staring at our conjoined hands like they're going to combust any minute. The way we fit together, the rough callousness from his palms and the heat pulsing from his hand, feels nothing but right.

I flick my eyes up to his and watch the way his pupils dilate when I stroke my thumb gently on top of his. Deep, slow breaths. Tight jaw ticking. He's fucking beautiful, and it takes everything in me not to lean in and claim those lips for myself again.

"Those were your parents outside the hotel," I manage with a rough swallow of my throat.

I can tell his mood is shot to hell from whatever confrontation happened earlier. Maybe with his walls lowered, I can sneak over the threshold and get this man to soften up for me.

Will nods, his eyes fixed on our hands. I keep tracing slow circles over his thumb, grounding him to me.

"So that was Jameson Sinclair," I say.

"The one and only."

"You seem close."

A sudden snort escapes him. I grin wide as he hides his mouth behind his hand, laughter spilling out anyway. God, it's the best sound I've ever heard.

It rumbles in his throat before breaking loose from his chest, and I can't help laughing with him. Laughter looks sexy on Will Sinclair.

"Yeah. That man is my best friend," Will says, still chuckling, lips curved in a way that makes it impossible to look anywhere else.

When the humor fades, his face turns almost somber, and he squeezes my hand tighter. "We're far from close, War. Every time I see him, my vision goes red."

Asking what happened between them or what they were even doing here in the first place is on the tip of my tongue, but I tread lightly, knowing this is the most vulnerable he's ever been with me. I'm not one to walk on eggshells; I sort of bulldoze my way into everything—obnoxious, loud, and at times annoying. But for some weird reason, Will has my brain working overtime, actually considering my words before I blurt them out.

"My father was doing his usual bullshit. With our annual family gala coming up in a few months, he was griping on making sure I bring a sensible date because I have a reputation to uphold. Fucking annoying."

"Family gala?"

Will scrubs a hand over his face. "Yeah . . . It's, uh . . . it's something we do every year for . . ." Will stammers, struggling to get out the words that seem to be stuck in his throat.

He's frazzled, and while usually I'd capitalize on this to make a joke, I pivot the conversation to help him out.

"And your mother?"

"My mother, well . . ." He scoffs. "She's just as bad as he is. They're nothing like your family, Brooks."

Something in my heart cracks at the mention of my family. If it were my parents waiting outside my hotel, there'd be a lot of screaming, hugging, and kissing. Yes, my mom and dad still kiss me on the lips and I don't give a fuck.

Will can't even bring himself to look at his parents, let alone acknowledge them. No warmth. No color. No love.

I turn fully to face him, holding his eyes with genuine sincerity. Not pity, but honesty laid bare. "You're always welcome to my family, Sinclair. I know I give you shit, and I'm still pissed you've been dodging me." I pause. "But shitty parents don't erase the fact that you've got people who care. I care."

He sucks in a sharp breath, and it's almost like I'm imagining him leaning closer to me. The overwhelming scent of clove surrounds me—and holy shit.

He *is* leaning closer. And closer. And closer.

So close, his lips barely graze against mine, lighting every nerve on my body in a blazing trail of fire. Fuck it. Just a taste . . .

Knock, knock, knock. "Boys! Put your clothes back on! Coach needs us in the lobby in five!" Truett, my *ex-best friend*, shouts through the door, his snickers fading as he moves down the hall.

The moment's doused in ice-cold water, and our hands unlink from each other. Will clears his throat, standing from the bed.

"Uh, thanks . . . War. I'm gonna use the restroom. I'll meet you down at the lobby."

I move to stand, shoving my hands in my pockets to keep from reaching out to him. "Yup. You got it."

Will gives me a nod before nearly running to the bathroom and closing himself in.

I stare at the door, unable to stop my feet from taking me right up to the front of it. My fist lifts to knock, but before my knuckles can make contact, I put it back down.

Damn. *Moony eyes.*

11

WILLIAM

A Stroke of Luck

The home crowd's chants for my former teammate who is up to bat are deafening—what was once a thrilling sound now only fuels the fire for revenge raging inside me.

St. Louis had always been home for me, and playing in this stadium for this crowd was one of the only things that gave me purpose for far too long.

I still don't know who I am away from the mound, but I hopefully have a few seasons left in me before I need to figure that out.

Digging my cleat into the dirt, I bend forward and narrow my sight to see which pitch Brooks is going to call for.

Fastball.

Fuck that.

I shake him off, and he cracks his neck in annoyance before giving me the sign for a slider.

Nodding, I stand upright and bring my glove up to my face to hide the seams of the ball.

My eyes stray of their own volition to the owner's box my parents are sitting in directly behind home plate, giving them the best view in the stadium.

Good. I hope he hasn't missed a second of the asswhooping his team has received from me and my teammates tonight.

Pride for my formidable performance swells in my chest, mixing with the fury I've been feeling since the old man practically ambushed me outside our hotel earlier.

A bead of sweat drips down my forehead, narrowly missing my eye as I throw a slider that veers to the right, causing my former teammate to swing and miss just like I knew he would.

Strike two.

With two outs in the bottom of the ninth, I'm one out away from a perfect game.

Possibly one pitch away.

Instead of throwing the ball back to me, Warren jogs from the plate to the mound to hand me the ball. Bringing his catcher's mitt up to cover his mouth, he murmurs for only me to hear, "I can't think of a bigger 'fuck you' to your dad than throwing your first perfect game against his team. What do you say, Sinclair? You ready to finish this?"

I nod once, too focused on the task at hand to talk to him right now.

"I say you throw your curve," Brooks suggests.

Shaking my head, I bring my own glove up to cover my mouth so my lips can't be read. "He's always been able to hit my curve. I'm throwing another slider. He's not expecting me to throw another one, and DeLuca has never touched it."

Brooks' gaze bounces between my eyes, and he must see the determination set in them because he says, "I'm good with that. Give him hell." With a slap on my shoulder, Brooks puts the ball in my glove and jogs back to behind the plate.

For appearances sake, he gives me a sign I shake off, then another that I nod my head to. It's go time. One last slider and maybe I'll do what only twenty-four other pitchers have done before me.

Throw a perfect game.

It's something I've only dreamt of, knowing it was a long shot—an anomaly—to be able to actually do so in the major league.

Wiping my face across the shoulder of my jersey, I take a deep breath and stand to my full height.

With my weight on my back leg, I wind up and release, transferring all of my weight to my front leg. I watch in anxious desperation as the ball leaves my hand and veers off to the right for a second time just as DeLuca swings and misses without making contact.

Strike three.

Out number three.

Holy shit.

I did it.

I fucking did it!

My first perfect game.

This is monumental—once in a lifetime.

"Let's fucking go, baby! That's what I'm talkin' about!" Brooks shouts as he throws off his catcher's mask and mitt before charging the mound. He tackles me in an embrace, but I manage to keep us from falling to the ground.

His chest heaves against mine, matching my heavy breathing. My heart rate picks up speed, and my body heats from the feel of his sweat-slicked skin against mine.

He grips the sides of my face in his hands and screams, "Let's fuckin' go! You did it!"

Tension builds between us as his gaze flits between my eyes and my lips.

The brief, heated moment is broken as our teammates join us, slapping me on the back and giving me congratulatory high fives.

Brooks backs away to give our teammates space to embrace me, though my stare doesn't stray from his. Our intense exchange leaves me with a hunger I'm not sure can be satiated by anyone but him.

"Alright, man, I'm hitting the showers," I tell Mateo, slapping him on the back as I pass by him.

"I'm headed out to the bus. Great game, Sinclair. I owe you a drink when we get to Chicago."

"Thanks, Costa. See you out there." What I don't tell him is I won't be taking him up on that drink. If I have it my way, I won't be leaving my hotel room this evening after we check in. I won't even try to blame it on the fact that we're on a brutal long stretch of away games. No, it's got everything to do with my catcher who just so happens to be standing with his back to me in the shower stall across from where I stand.

I *should* turn around and look away. I *shouldn't* be staring at the way the water pelts off the broad muscles of his traps. And I should absolutely *not* be following the trails of droplets as they run down his corded back to his supple butt and thick catcher's thighs.

Need like I've never known surges inside of me, threatening to pull me under.

What is happening to me?

Squeezing my eyes shut, I curse myself for staring at my teammate—at another man. When I open them, I'm stunned to find Brooks not only facing me, but blatantly taking me in with a salacious smile.

"Why is it that I'm always catching you with your eyes on me, Pretty Boy?" he rasps, his voice pure smoke. "You like what you see?"

Fighting like hell to keep my eyes on his, I'm pleased with my restraint. That is . . . until I watch his hand glide over his chest, lathering his tanned, tattooed skin with his body wash, the citrus and pine scents permeating the dense air between us. My self-control slips, my gaze remaining fixated on his hand as it coasts past the contours of his abs straight to his fully erect length.

Look away. Turn the fuck away. Even as I shout the commands to myself, I can't seem to break my stare.

I'm far too entranced watching the way the corded muscles of his forearm flex as he fists his thick cock in his hand, giving it a firm stroke. He shamelessly pulls his bottom lip between his teeth as he continues to work his fist up and down his shaft.

My vision blurs at the edges, and I have to grip the tiled wall beside me as I fight off the arousal that would surely consume me if I gave into it.

"I think about it far more than I should, you know."

"Think about what?" I finally ask, my low voice sounding foreign to me.

"What you'd look like if you stopped being such a stiff and let go." He hisses through his teeth as his hand begins to work harder, and I can't help but stare as he does so. "God, I bet you'd look so fuckin' good giving up control to me."

"Don't get your hopes up."

"Oh, yeah? And why do you say that?"

"I don't give up control."

"Maybe I'll make you lose that control you like to hold on to so tightly," he taunts. "I already make you *crazy*."

Narrowing my eyes, I step back into the water spray to wet my hair. When I grab my shampoo bottle, I tell him, "I wouldn't count on it if I were you. I submit to no one."

"Careful, Sinclair. I've never been one to shy away from a challenge, and that sounded like a hell of a challenge to me."

Turning my back to him, I mutter under my breath, "Only you would take that as a challenge."

By way of avoiding him, I take a longer shower than necessary, which is needed to come down from the adrenaline rush of pitching a perfect game.

I'm the last one onto the team bus, but no one gives me shit. Instead, the guys all shout their congratulations, many of them standing to pat me on the back as I pass them by in the aisle on my way toward the back of the bus.

My usual spot is occupied by none other than the man who has taken up far too much space in my mind.

"You're in my seat."

Without looking up from his phone, he murmurs, "I am."

"Why?"

"Because you just pitched a perfect game and I want to celebrate with you," he explains.

I sigh and set my duffle bag in the overhead compartment before taking the aisle seat beside him.

Once I'm situated, the aisle lights shut off and the faint dim of some overhead lights are the only thing to illuminate the darkened bus.

Before I can put on my noise canceling headphones, Brooks grabs my wrist to stop me.

I let out a grunt of frustration. "What is it?"

He leans into my space, lowering his voice when he says, "I said we're celebrating. Can't very well do that if you're ignoring me."

"And how do you intend to do that? We're on a team bus. It's not like we're at a bar and can have a drink to celebrate."

Brooks drags the back of his fingers down my forearm, eliciting goosebumps in their wake.

"My idea of celebrating was a bit more . . . *hands on* than grabbing drinks with teammates."

I nearly choke on my gasp as his hand moves to grasp my thigh.

What is he doing to me? And why am I dying to find out?

12

BROOKS

WHAT ARE YOU DOING TO ME?

ADRENALINE FROM THE WIN tonight is still ripping through my veins. Watching Will throw a perfect game was nothing short of admirable. Fucking epic. Hot as hell. Seems our heart-to-heart earlier at the hotel brought us luck tonight.

I'm amped up, lust and desire taking over my body, moving like molten lava. My hand on Will's thigh tightens, his gasp causing a twitch beneath my sweatpants.

My cock has been throbbing since the post-game shower. Couldn't help myself knowing his eyes were on me—wanting me. His eyes always fucking on me. It's not the fact that the tension between us is real, or that he's a household name in the league and I've looked up to him since I owned my first mitt.

It's this look he gives me. A look I've noticed that's only for me. Molten, deadly midnight blue that pierces straight through me every damn time. It's a look that ruins my resolve, makes me fucking hard, and straight up drives me crazy.

Ha. Looks like Sin makes me crazy, too.

He's giving me the look right now. And I want to push him. Punish him for avoiding me. For denying that the kiss between us didn't mean shit. Bull fucking shit, Sinclair.

The bus is dark, and most of our teammates are about to fall asleep or have headphones in. We're not in the very last row, but far enough back where the majority of everyone is in front of us. With a covert glance over my shoulder, all I see are closed eyes and hoods up over heads.

Perfect.

Leaning in toward Will, I lightly brush my lips along the shell of his ear and whisper, "Do you want me to stop?"

The hand I have gripped around his muscular thigh drags higher ever so slowly, and I take my time feeling the sinew of muscles through the fabric of his sweatpants. So firm and tight, making me want to take my time to work out the kinks and get him to relax.

But my idea of relaxation right now has everything to do with the direction in which my hand is moving. Up, up, and up.

Will's lack of words and speed in his breathing gives me my answer. His eyes are wild, filled with unadulterated lust as he frantically darts his gaze throughout the bus. It's quiet, only the steady sound of the bus engine and muted music from earbuds.

My pinky brushes the outline of his cock. I tease his erection, barely grazing against it with my fingers, reveling in the way he squirms and softly grunts in his seat.

I palm his thick dick, squeezing once before slipping my fingers up underneath the hem of his hoodie. When I pull on his waistband, his eyes flit to me with bewilderment, blacked-out pupils staring back at me with nothing but heat in them.

I'm so hard it hurts. The cover of darkness helps hide the tent I'm currently pitching, but I throb and ache between my legs, and my balls feel so damn heavy I could curse this pretty boy for making me like this.

You make me crazy.

I'm breathing hard in his ear, finding his gloriously thick cock and gripping it tight in my grasp.

"Commando, huh?" I muse, lips tilting into a devilish smirk. "You thought about this, didn't you? Giving me easy access to your fucking dick. Fuck, that's hot."

His jaw tightens the second I squeeze, and I use my thumb to swipe the bead of precum seeping out, spreading it over the tip of him.

Will groans quietly, his eyes rolling back when I give him a long stroke from base to tip. I don't remember the last time I gave a proper handjob. Most of the men I've hooked up with prefer blowjobs or just straight to fucking. But I'm going to make this so good for him—make it last for him. Tease him.

"That feel good, Sin? You like it when I stroke you like this?" I murmur, nibbling his earlobe as I work him so, so slowly. Up and down.

His expression morphs from feral need to annoyed, back to un-tamed lust in a matter of three strokes of his cock. I've got him melting in the palm of my hand, and fuck—if that doesn't feed my ego.

"What are you doing to me?" Will breathes against my mouth.

Looks like he no longer cares if anyone's watching. The thought of getting caught only makes me leak and stroke him harder. Just knowing a set of curious eyes could be watching Will's face morph into twisted pleasure is enough to almost make me fuckin' bust.

Will's hand suddenly grips my thigh. I don't dare stop my minis-trations despite the painful throb between my legs. "I bet you won't do it," I grit, loving the heat from his hand searing me through my sweats.

I earn a rare smirk that makes him look laid back and boyish, a welcome change from his signature scowl.

Will wastes no time snaking his hand past my waistband and straight to the Promised Land. His rough hand explores my inches from the tip of my leaking slit, all the way down to the tuft of hair near the base where he slightly tugs. I growl quietly into his neck, stroking him with a little more urgency.

"I bet I can make you come first," Will rasps, surprising me and lighting me on fire at the same time.

Before I can give him a snarky response, he's jacking me off with vigor, determined to get me to blow my load with a bus full of people. Nothing excites me more than a challenge, but a challenge from Will Sinclair? Sign me the fuck up.

Our foreheads press together, both of us panting heavily against our lips. I start to lose control, feeling the familiar tightening in my balls.

Shit. Shit. Shit.

"Oh, you're close, aren't you, War? You want me that bad, baby?"

Baby? Let me off this fucking bus so I can show him exactly how bad I want him. I'll tear his clothes off like a rabid animal and get so lost deep inside of him he won't even remember his goddamn name.

"I want you to come is what I want, Sin."

"You gotta do better than that." He strains each word as I feel his cock thickening in my hand.

"I can hold out." I struggle, my breath stuck in my throat as I withhold my impending orgasm.

Fucking shit!

"No you can't. I need you to come for me now, War. Do it."

Jesus. His dirty talk is about to send me over the edge. Who knew that Pretty Boy had such a filthy mouth.

"You fucking do it," I quip back.

I swear the veins in my neck are going to explode, sweat dotting along my upper lip. Will stares at my mouth, his face lit with the moonlight coming from the window. He's all consuming and so fucking gorgeous it physically hurts. I'm barely holding on, begging—wishing—he'd lick my mouth and taste how badly I need his release.

His hand feels fucking glorious. We stroke each other hard, both of us twisting and tugging as if we were getting ourselves off. But it's his rough hand on me, bringing me so close to a climax he's working hard for, that makes me almost want to give it to him.

But nah. I won't yield so easily. He wants me to come? He needs to work a little harder to get me there.

"Give me your mouth, Sin."

"W-what?" he stutters, breathless.

His hand doesn't slow, pricking my skin and giving me the god-damn tingles again.

"You keep staring at my mouth. Give me yours and I'll give you another taste."

Before I can give another stroke, his mouth collides with mine, and that does me in. He swallows my restrained moan, and I savor his taste like I'll never have it again. I'm so lost in my climax I don't realize my hand is covered in warm, sticky liquid.

Will's tongue battles with mine, and we devour each other under the quiet cloak of darkness with an entire audience around us. We both work each other over through our powerful orgasms, licking and biting our lips, unable to pull away from the intoxicating taste of lust.

"Holy shit," I pant against his mouth, rolling my damp forehead over his as I regain feeling in my body.

"I won," Will taunts, giving me another sexy smirk.

I silently chuckle, slowly pulling my hand out of his sweats. He does the same. "No way. It was a tie."

With his clean hand, he pulls a rag out of his backpack, cleaning off his other. He hands it off to me and I follow.

"Don't be a sore loser, War."

"Fine," I whisper, leaning in to claim his lips in a soft kiss. "You win."

13

WILLIAM

City After City of Denial

Chicago

War:

Tell me what you're wearing.

Me:

My uniform?

Me:

Shouldn't you be getting ready for the game?

War:

I am. I'm practicing my new pregame ritual.

Me:

And that is?

War:

Do you really wanna know?

Me:

Please. Don't keep me in suspense.

War:

Jacking off to the thought of you coming for me.

War:

Have you ever seen yourself while you're coming undone?

War:

Fucking mesmerizing.

Me:

See you at the game…

War:

Still a stiff I see.

Cincinnati

War:

Have you ever had a crush on a fictional character?

Me:

wtf?

War:

Humor me.

Me:

Have you?

War:

I asked you first.

War:

Quit being a brat (that's my job) and answer the
question.

Me:

A fictional character being what? Like an actor?

War:

A cartoon character, specifically.

Me:

WHAT THE FUCK IS WRONG WITH YOU?!

War:

Oh, I can see I've struck a nerve.

War:

It must be a good character. Hmm… now I'm fully invested. Who is it?

Me:

You're mental.

War:

Fine. I'll go first.

War:

It's a toss up between Li Shang from *Mulan* and Prince Eric from *The Little Mermaid*.

Me:

Did you always know you were into guys?

War:

Yes, and women. Jessica Rabbit got me right along with Lola Bunny *face sweating emoji*

Me:

I was more of a Princess Jasmine guy. Come to think of it, Jade kind of looks like her …

War:

MY SISTER??????????

Me:

Yeah. The Warren black hair just does it for me.

War:

YOU'RE SICK.

War:

DON'T EVER TALK ABOUT HER AGAIN.

War:

You're not invited back to my family's dinners if you don't take it back.

War:

I don't care if my dad worships the ground you walk on.

Me:

Alright, I take it back.

Me:

But only because your mom's cooking is to die for.

War:

I didn't even get to show you my childhood bedroom while you were there.

Me:

Is my poster still on the wall?

War:

Fuck, I think it is.

War:

I should grab that and put it on my ceiling for nights when I'm feeling lonely.

Me:

I'm sure you're awfully lonely right now considering we all got our own rooms on this trip.

War:

Nah, I'm excited to get a good night's sleep sans your snoring.

Me:

Fuck right off. I don't snore.

War:

Oh, but you do, Pretty Boy. You'd think with that big contract of yours you could afford to see an ENT. Gotta be a deviated septum or something causing you to saw logs so loud every night.

Me:

I've literally never had another teammate tell me I snore.

War:

About that… Am I your favorite roomie you've ever had?

Me:

Depends on the day.

Milwaukee

War:

What's your go-to karaoke song?

Me:

Never sang karaoke.

War:

You're kidding, right?

Me:

No.

War:

Leave it up to me to show you all the finer things in life.

War:

Since you asked… Mine would definitely be "All The Small Things" by Blink 182.

Me:

Never heard it.

War:

What. The. Fuck.

War:

Did you live under a rock when you grew up???

Me:

I'm joking obviously.

War:

Thank God.

War:

Fine, what do you listen to before a game?

Me:

I typically have a playlist of Aerosmith, Bon Jovi, ACDC, and Queen going before a game.

War:

OK, I can fuck with that.

War:

Now if I made you sing karaoke with me, which song would you choose?

Me:

"Wanted Dead Or Alive" by Bon Jovi.

War:

FUCK! That's a good one.

Me:

I guess it's a toss up between that or "Pour Some Sugar On Me" by Def Leppard.

War:

You tryin' to tell me something, Sin?

Me:

IDK am I?

14
WILLIAM

Dismissed

HANGING MY HEAD, THE sounds of my steps echo off the concrete floors and walls of the tunnel as I head for the exit of Milwaukee's stadium.

We lost tonight and I played like absolute shit, giving up four runs before Coach finally pulled me. Not only were Brooks and I off-sync, but I just couldn't get my head in the game.

After a couple weeks of playful banter and back and forth flirting via text messages, Brooks and I haven't discussed what happened between us on the bus.

It's not that he's avoiding talking to me, or what happened between us, but we also haven't discussed it.

It was exhilarating, the threat of being caught by one of our teammates while our hands were fisted on each other's cocks. And while I can't find it in myself to regret what happened, I am pissed I'm letting it affect my game.

My blood rushes south just thinking about that night. It's not only the first time I've been intimately touched by a man, but it's the first time I've touched one as well.

Which is why my lust-induced high is plummeting at a faster rate with each day Brooks avoids talking about it. I get that I was the first one to ignore him after our kiss, and maybe this is him getting me back. If this is his way of punishing me, consider me punished. I don't like the way it feels to be on the receiving end of the avoidance.

"Sinclair, wait up!" Brooks shouts.

I pause midstep, my shoulders stiffening momentarily before I glance over my shoulder and see Brooks trying to catch up to me. I take a deep breath when I see him hot on my heels.

I turn to face him. "Warren," I grit, feigning a nonchalance I definitely don't feel at the moment.

"Hey," he says, a little breathless. "You okay?"

"I'm fine."

"Bullshit." He laughs. "Was it the game? I know we weren't as in tune with each other tonight, but don't sweat it. We'll get our groove back next time."

It's hard to stay frustrated with Brooks when he's so damn positive all the time. He felt we were off tonight, thinking it had everything to do with the game. But how can I tell him that it has everything to do with him?

How the hell do I approach the subject of what happened between us the other night? When I'm on the mound, everyone sees me taking Brooks' calls like I do every week. But what they don't see is the way I trace the veins in his forearms with my eyes when he flexes. Or how he smirks behind his mask when he knows I'm about to strike someone out.

Something is brewing between us. And I need him to say it out loud because clearly—I don't know how.

Instead of trying to sort through what I'm feeling, I give him bullshit as my default answer. "I know this team got used to losing last season, but I haven't made my career into what it is by playing like shit. Every game counts. Every pitch of mine matters."

"It's not that serious. We still have plenty of season left to pl—"

"This has nothing to do with the fucking season." I snap at him, my tone biting.

Brooks' face morphs with confusion, but then his eyes soften as he searches my face for some sort of clarity.

"Alright, then talk to me. What's this about?"

I scoff, unable to stop myself from rolling my eyes. "Oh, now you want to talk."

In typical Brooks Warren fashion, he laughs, throwing his head back like I've just told the most hilarious joke of the century.

"You're a moody motherfucker, you know that? Now tell me what I've done to make you pissy."

I'm berating myself for not being able to get a hold of my emotions. This man has a way of burrowing himself so far into my head, I can't think straight. Literally.

Everyday since he barrelled into my life, it's hard to tell left from right, or up from down. My entire world turned inside out, and now my every waking thought is consumed with Brooks' laugh and the way I feel when he touches me.

Fine. If he can't read between the lines, I'll just say it. "Why are you avoiding it?"

"*It* being?" He quirks a brow.

"The other night. On the bus," I reply in a hushed tone.

"I'm not."

"Don't you think we should talk about it?"

He shrugs. "Not really. I mean, what's there to talk about? I blew your world, and you blew your load all over my hand."

"You say that as if you didn't do that exact same thing," I deadpan.

"My apologies. We blew our loads on each other's hands, and you most definitely blew my mind and world." Brooks smirks.

I step impossibly closer to him, lowering my voice. "And the reason you've been avoiding talking about it is?"

An adorably bashful look crosses his face, and for a moment I forget why I'm in a pissy mood to begin with. "Well . . ." He rubs the back of his neck. "That was a big night for us. I didn't want to push you further."

I huff out a sigh of resignation and shake my head. "Now you want to be a man of virtue?"

"When have I pushed you beyond what you've wanted?" he questions, which seemingly puts out my fire—because the truth is, he hasn't pushed me. I've wanted everything we've done thus far, whether I was ready to admit it at the time or not.

"That's beside the point," I grumble.

"Then what's your point?"

I open my mouth to reply, but then out of the corner of my eye, I see Mateo sauntering down the tunnel toward us. He doesn't say anything, whistling like he doesn't have a care in the world. But as he passes the two of us, he does a double take and winks like he's somehow in on our secret. The look on his face unsettles me.

Clenching my jaw, I try to quell the anxiety swirling in the pit of my stomach before replying to Brooks. "My point is why now? Why do you all of a sudden choose now—after what we did the other night—not to push me."

"You want me to push you? Huh?" He swipes his thumb against his bottom lip. "Because it sure sounds like it, Sin." Brooks ignores the fact that we can be seen by our teammates, and he crowds my space, backing me up against the cinderblock wall of the hallway.

I swallow past the thickness of desire coating my throat. "Let's say I do. What happens then?"

He lets out a low chuckle that rumbles in his chest, causing it to vibrate against my own. Shit, just the sound of his laughter has me turned on. "Then"—he pauses to look me up and down—"we go back to our hotel room and you set the pace."

"I set the pace?" I question, feeling hesitant all of a sudden at the thought of where this will likely lead.

"Without question. Anything we do is because you say so. I'll obey your every command like a good boy."

Fuck. My dick twitches beneath my zipper just thinking about all the possibilities.

I fight the urge to lean in and press my lips against his, knowing we're not alone at the moment. But once we get in our hotel room, all bets are off. I'm done pretending I'm unaffected by what happened the other night on the bus.

Instead of kissing him the way I'm dying to, we step away from each other and walk outside toward the bus when a fan starts to shout, "Brooks! Oh my gosh! Brooks, do you remember me?"

He looks over his shoulder at the woman with light brown hair down to her waist and curves any man would kill to touch. Recognition sets in his features, and he shoots her a smile. "I do."

The fact that he does indeed remember her causes her to bite her lip seductively. "I was thinking we could rekindle our night of fun together. Got any teammates who would be down?"

"I do, but I don't know if tonight's gonna be that night, sweetheart," he tells her, and I'm not sure what to make of that response.

There's something extremely terrifying yet exciting at the thought of having Brooks all to myself. But my mind betrays me, planting seeds of doubt. Maybe it'll be easier to have this woman as a buffer so I can have Brooks again without fully committing to something I might not be ready for.

"Why not?" I ask, which causes Brooks to look over his shoulder at me in question.

What are you doing? he mouths to me.

I lean in behind him, whispering in his ear, "Wasn't it you who said everything's better in threes?"

Brooks pins me with a hard stare, almost expecting me to say no—urging me to drop this. But I don't.

Shrugging my shoulders, I feign nonchalance, and his brows wrinkle. I give him an assured nod, though I'm feeling anything but.

Instead of letting him do the talking, I tell the woman, "Why don't you meet us at our hotel and we'll show you a hell of a good time."

Her face lights up. "Name the place and I'm there."

"You sure about this?" Brooks says just loud enough for only me to hear.

"You said I set the pace, right?" I tell him, trying to keep the shakiness out of my voice.

Brooks takes a beat, his mossy gaze searing into mine. Finally, he turns toward the woman with a fixed smile. "We're staying at the Interstellar Hotel. See you soon," he tells her, his voice withdrawn and sounding anything but enthusiastic before he turns and makes his way onto the team bus.

Once we're seated, he wastes no time turning to look at me. "Are you into her?"

"I mean, I am into women, yes," I drawl.

He scoffs in frustration. "You know that's not what I meant."

"I don't know. I guess so." I shrug, completely unaffected again, and it seems to piss him off.

Regret churns heavy in my stomach. What am I doing? Why the fuck did I invite her? It's not like I'm even into her. Sure, she's beautiful and probably great in bed. If anything, I pushed for this to see what Brooks would say because I was jealous of the fact that he's done this with her before, only he shared her with someone else.

Which has me questioning which of our teammates he's shared with in the past.

I stew on those thoughts the entire way back to the hotel, so in my own head I don't even realize we've arrived until Brooks nudges me on the shoulder to stand up.

"Let's go, Pretty Boy. We're the last ones left. Unless you've got a case of cold feet," he taunts, propelling me forward.

Adjusting the collar of my dress shirt, I assure him. "Not at all."

I'm sure he can see right through my bullshit act of being impervious.

Yet here we fucking go. What is wrong with me? Just when I thought I could maybe do this, I'm right back to square one. With hidden desires and a woman between us to mask them. And I've got no one but myself to blame.

Get your shit together, Sinclair.

The woman from the stadium—shit, I'm not even sure I caught her name—stands in the hotel lobby waiting for us.

I don't know how I missed it before, but she's wearing a WARREN jersey accompanied by the shortest pair of jean shorts, showcasing her long, toned legs.

She's sexy, there's no doubting that. But something snaps inside me seeing his last name across her back.

And when he leads her to the elevator, placing his large hand just above her ass, my vision clouds red.

I press against the far wall of the elevator, watching with insane jealousy as Brooks brushes her long hair to the side, almost taunting me with his name and number. He probably thinks he's being cheeky about the fact that she's a fan of his and isn't wearing my jersey.

But what he doesn't realize is something foreign starts to awaken deep in my chest. A white hot jealousy I've never felt before. It sears through me like a hot branding iron, and I'm feeling the walls of the elevator closing in. My vision tunnels on his fucking name over and over again.

Warren. Warren. Warren. *FUCKING MINE.*

Brooks looks my way, and I'm sure I'm doing a shit job of schooling my features if the way he's looking at me is anything to go off of.

Whatever expression he reads on my face has a frown forming on his. Now he looks almost unsure of himself as he steps back from the woman and sidesteps so he's merely an inch from me.

Leaning in, Brooks brushes his pinky against my hand, eliciting a chill to run up my arm and down my spine. In a hushed tone, he murmurs, "If you don't want this to happen, speak up and it ends now. But I'll do it if this is the only way I can have you."

I don't want a woman between us.

Instead of admitting that out loud, I tell him, "Tell her to leave."

"What?"

"Dismiss her," I hiss between clenched teeth.

"Why?" he questions, and at this point I think he's prodding me to open up more.

So I do just that. Turning to him, I disregard the fact that we're not alone and cup his cheek in my hand. "You know why. I'm done pretending we need someone between us. I don't want to share you anymore. I'm done sharing."

"Fuckin' finally," he rasps as the elevator arrives on our floor.

Confusion whirs to life when he leads her out of the elevator, down the hall toward our room.

"Wait here," he tells me when we're outside our hotel room door.

I do as he says, watching from the middle of the opening as Brooks walks her down the hall to another door and tells her, "Change of plans, darlin'."

Mateo opens the door, and they have a brief exchange while the woman stands in the doorway beside him. Mateo hangs his head out his door and wolf whistles as Brooks makes a beeline back to me.

Without uttering a single word, he pauses only momentarily to get a read on my expression. A single nod is all it takes for our lips to crash together as our bodies collide against the door.

We're out in the open again, where anyone could catch sight of us. It's thrilling—but reckless.

Brooks must read my thoughts because he reaches into my back pocket for the keycard to get us away from potentially prying eyes.

As soon as we're closed inside our room, we pick up right where we left off. Stripping each other from our clothes, he kisses me fervently, bringing my desire to a pinnacle.

We're ravenous in the way we're making out, taking what we want from the other as we roughly stroke each other's cocks.

Brooks breaks the kiss, his chest heaving as he pants, "I was hoping you'd tell her to leave."

I pause to really take him in. His lustrous eyes have darkened to a hunter green, and his inky hair is tousled from where I've already run my fingers through it. He's so alluring when he's turned on—everything about him pulls me in. So it's no wonder I lose control of my tongue and blurt, "Maybe we can do more."

Brooks looks momentarily taken aback, his eyes flicking back and forth between mine. Whatever he sees in my heated gaze must be consent enough for him because he leads me back to the edge of the bed, and then his lips are back on mine.

We're a pair of crazed souls hastily kissing each other.

Brooks licks a line down my jaw before sucking on my neck. He continues kissing, sucking, and biting his way down my body, worshipping every line and divet, pausing only to lick my belly button and bite each of my hips.

He kisses so far down, he's on his knees and biting into my thighs, touching every square inch of my skin except the one place I want him most.

Glancing up at me from his knees, we exchange a look, and I know he's waiting for permission. With my hands tangled in Brooks' hair, I tug hard at the nape of his neck.

"More?" he asks, his voice full of gravel.

I lick my lips and swallow hard past any uncertainty, giving him a single nod.

Brooks doesn't hesitate to grab my throbbing length in his hand as he slowly drags his tongue from the base of my cock to the tip. He licks at a frustratingly slow pace, torturously teasing me like the brat he is. Lapping up the precum leaking from my tip like a spout, he whimpers as he gets his first taste of me.

"More," I growl, voicing my need for him, causing a switch to flip in him. Brooks goes from teasing to ravenously taking me all the way to the back of his throat in a matter of seconds.

We groan in unison, the sound vibrating off the walls. But I couldn't fucking care less who hears—at this point, I'm too far gone. My balls tighten from the sounds escaping him as he sloppily works my cock in and out of his mouth.

He works me over, giving me the most insane blowjob—easily the best I've ever had. His mouth is warm and wet, his throat tight without the pause of a gag reflex, and I'm not sure how much longer I can take before I blow my load embarrassingly fast.

With my hands in his hair, I throw my head back and hiss when he takes every inch of me, something no one has ever been able to do before.

"Fuck! *Baby*. Yes, just like that," I encourage him as I hold my position at the back of his throat before snapping my hips back to allow him a second to breathe. Brooks whimpers, and I can't be sure if it's from me calling him baby again or if it's from the loss of me.

Either way, I'm desperate to hear that sound over and over again—it's a drug hit straight to my veins.

"You like that, huh? Taking my thick cock to the back of your throat. You're desperate for it, aren't you? Look at you," I marvel, taking him in on his knees as he worships the fuck out of every inch of my body.

Nudging his lips, I watch with utter fascination as he opens for me and licks the tip before moving to my balls and taking them in his mouth with a boldness I only wish I could possess.

"Oh, shit," I hiss, throwing my head back in pure ecstasy again.

Brooks releases my balls and growls, "Eyes on me, Pretty Boy. Always."

My head snaps down and I narrow my gaze on him. "So needy." I can't help the chuckle that escapes when he just shrugs, completely unashamed of the fact that he is indeed needy as fuck when it comes to my attention.

My laughter comes to an abrupt halt when he continues his min-istrations, cupping my balls in his hands as he uses his teeth ever so slightly, just enough to drive me crazy.

"That's it, baby. You're doing so good," I praise through gritted teeth.

He whimpers again, and I feel like I've just won the league MVP earning that sound from him.

Brooks pops off my dick, a string of spit hanging from his lips as he asks, "Can I try something?"

I quirk a brow in response.

"Do you trust me?"

Undoubtedly.

Instead of answering with that, I roughly clear my throat. "Yeah."

Without another word, Brooks pushes me back onto the bed, manhandling me a bit until my head rests just in front of the head-board.

Nudging his way between my thighs, he says, "Keep these spread open for me."

I do as he says, though this position has me feeling vulnerable with how bared to him I am.

Trailing his tongue from the tip of my cock down the length to my balls, he grabs me by the backs of my knees and pulls me closer to him, holding me open even more.

With his eyes locked on mine, he spits straight onto the tight ring of my ass before lowering his mouth to that very spot and dragging his tongue in a slow circle, causing me to buck my hips off the bed.

"Just relax. I promise I'll make it feel so good for you," he urges before picking right back up where he left off and fulfilling that very promise while driving his hips into the bed, essentially fucking the mattress. A fantasy of it being me he's driving into clouds my vision and has me unraveling at the seams.

Oh fuck. Why is this the single greatest thing I've ever felt in my life?

Scratch that—Brooks erases that thought when he one-ups himself, fisting my cock in his hand while continuing to lick a trail from my balls to my ass. I let out a feral growl I'm sure can be heard throughout the hotel when his tongue dips just inside the untouched ring.

"Holy *fuuuuck*! Dear God!"

Brooks chuckles deep in his chest. "God won't help you here, Sin."

The sight of Brooks propped up on one elbow with his arm wrapped around my thigh while sucking the pointer finger of his other hand into his mouth is sexy as sin, but when he takes it out with an audible pop and uses it to prod just the tip into my ass, I can't stop the grunt of approval that slips free.

And when he takes me deep into the back of his throat again, the combination is sensory overload. Pleasure I've never felt has my senses going haywire, and before I can give him any warning, I'm coming down his throat with a force I've never felt. White dots spot my vision to the point I think I'll pass out, and I thank God I'm lying down right now.

Propping myself up on my elbows, I stare down at him while my chest heaves for air. There's a drop of my cum dripping down his chin, causing a fierce desire to claim him—possess him.

He comes to a kneeling position between my legs and fiercely grips his length.

"Tell me who makes you crazy," he commands, his voice gravelled yet breathless.

"You do."

"Say it again," he hisses.

"You make me fucking crazy, baby."

Brooks moans, driving my one thigh back with his free hand, while fisting his cock in the other, vigorously pumping his length until streams of his cum paint my ass. The feeling of his release seeping into my asshole is depraved yet addicting all at the same time.

Falling onto me, I welcome his weight as we fight to catch our breath and come down from our mutual high.

Best fucking blowjob ever.

"Why thank you," Brooks replies through a fit of laughter.

I cover my face with my forearm in embarrassment. "Shit. I said that out loud, didn't I?"

"Sure fuckin' did."

"Whatever. I can't even find it in me to be ashamed to admit it."

15

BROOKS

Greedy Boy

I'VE NEVER FELT SUCH insatiable lust. No one else has ever managed to capture my attention the way he has. As much as I hate to admit, I've been around the block. I like to fuck—sue me.

But something about how Will only laughs when he's around me and no one else, or how he ends up in my bed when we're on a stretch of away games, making out like goddamn teenagers and touching each other like we can't get enough . . . I want more. I *need* more.

We haven't gone further than kissing and mind-blowing hand-jobs. Well, and me taking him in my mouth countless times. Which is totally fine with me. I know Will avoids talking about his sexuality, and in that regard, I don't push him.

If anything, we're turning out to be pretty good friends. Friends who give each other orgasms. It's even gone so far as me helping Pretty Boy move into his new cushy beach house in Coronado. We make great use of his bed and the balcony connected to his bedroom. Turns out he grows a steel rod at the thought of being watched, pushing me to my knees out in the open air as I swallow him down.

For weeks now, we've spent almost all of our free time away from baseball together. Early morning runs on the beach, surfing lessons I secretly enjoy giving him, and chill nights with the teammates at the bar to play pool or darts.

At times, it's hard to transition from how we act in private to being public figures out on the field. Since the night of our kiss, everything between us has changed. If I'm being truthful with myself, it actually changed weeks before that. Probably from the moment he walked into our locker room, looking straight out of a Ralph Lauren campaign.

That was months ago, but watching him now as he stands in front of his locker, stripping out of his practice clothes with sweat still clinging to every inch of his skin, sends a spark straight through my chest.

We had pitcher-catcher practice today, but of course Pretty Boy needed to put extra work in and kept me behind. I'm not complaining, though. Three months ago, I would've bitched come hell or high water at needing to spend any extra time with someone who annoyed the shit out of me.

Oh, how the tables have turned.

We practiced some new signals, and of course I had to add a few secret ones only for him. I don't know what he's doing to me. I'm giddy like a schoolgirl skipping around with a new crush. I haven't even had a craving for women, let alone any other man.

"Now who's the one with the wandering eyes?" Will teases, glancing at me over his shoulder with a smirk.

"Now that I know exactly how that ass looks underneath your pants, I take my fill anytime I want."

It's true. I find myself staring at the perfection of Will's hard planes and sculpted muscles day in and day out. No shame in my game. My cock stirs when Will strips completely naked, tossing me heated looks as his half-hard dick lays perfectly against his thigh.

Thank God we're the only two left here. The way he struts toward the showers with his ass muscles flexing in each step has me panting like a dog. He knows what he's doing, and I love the confidence growing within him each time we're together.

He may not be able to confess his true feelings, or come to terms with his sexuality, but it doesn't take a rocket scientist to figure out that Will Sinclair fucking wants me as much as I want him.

I peel off every article of clothing I have in a flash, following him into the steam of the shower. He's started without me, letting the water spill down his chest and shoulders in tantalizing rivulets.

With his back to me, I slowly approach him, pressing my erection between the valley of his ass. The heat from the water pales in comparison to the fire that ignites every time our bodies touch, an inferno of lust and insatiable need.

I bite his shoulder at the same time my hands snake around his waist. With splayed fingers, I let my fingertips memorize the ridges of his abs, softly tugging the tuft of hair right above his thick cock.

"You kept me out longer so you could get me all to yourself, didn't you," I rasp in his ear.

A hint of a devious grin plays on his lips. "You needed the extra work. I was just being a team player."

"Oh? You wanna be a team player, Sin?" I suck hard on his neck, tracing his veins with my tongue. One of my hands grips his girth, tugging once, then twice.

A low grumble erupts from his chest, and I bite his shoulder harder, leaving my teeth imprints on his heated skin.

"Get on your knees," I demand, my voice low and raspy in his ear.

Will has never taken me in his mouth before. All our time spent together, I've never expected him to return the favor by giving me a blowjob. But with each day, his trust for me grows. I don't take advantage of it, and I try not to take it for granted.

I told him myself we'd always take things at his pace. He sets the rhythm, and I follow willingly with no questions asked. But this moment feels different. I've gotten to know Will Sinclair intimately, physically, and emotionally in ways no one else has gotten access to.

Reading his body language is almost second-nature to me. I know when he's hungry, when he's angry, when he's fucking horny. His eyes don't hide from me, no matter how much he hides his heart.

He needs the push. Just a bit. *I'll push.*

When Will doesn't move, I repeat myself in a harsher tone. "You heard me. Get on your knees, Sin."

A beat passes, and then he turns around with a molten gaze that practically melts me on the spot.

Oh, he fucking wants this.

We take a step back out of the stream of the shower, where the water pelts his back as he slowly lowers himself onto the shower floor. I'd be concerned for his old man knees on this tile, but with how hard I am and how much I'm leaking, this won't take long at all.

I brush his damp hair back from his face, my hand lingering as I cup his cheek. My thumb slips past his lips, and heat rushes through me when his tongue circles it—his cheeks hollowing like he's already practicing what he plans to do to me.

My cock swings in front of Will, his eyes locked onto the precum seeping from the tip. There's something so primal in his gaze, like he wants to eat me alive. Not gonna lie, the power trip he's giving me is doing wonders for my ego. Pretty Boy on his knees for me. *Only me.*

"Stick your tongue out," I snarl, fighting every urge to drive my cock straight down his tight throat.

He obeys instantly. What a good boy. "So much for 'I submit to no one,'" I tease, catching the glower in Will's eyes.

I slap my cock on the flat of his tongue, using my hand to squeeze out drops of precum straight into his mouth. He hesitates for a moment, but then greedily laps up the beads of glossy liquid.

Will hums in pleasure, snapping something deep in my chest where a feral beast is ready to lash out and claim him. I can't wait any longer.

"Open wide and take me, Sinclair."

The moment his mouth parts, I press the head of my cock past his lips, my hand locking around his jaw as I guide the rest of my length down his throat.

Christ, that feels good.

My head tips up toward the ceiling, and I revel in the feeling of Will's mouth working me deeper. When I hit the back of his throat and he gags, I almost bust. "Fuck," I mutter, pulling back slightly to give him some reprieve.

But he's determined alright, taking me back in without missing a beat.

"Look at you. So fuckin' greedy."

He answers with a nibble on the head of my cock, and something about that makes me go insane. Gripping his jaw tighter, I show him no mercy and fuck into his mouth hard and fast.

Eyes watery and throat tightening, I'm in Nirvana. In and out, so, so goddamn good.

"Shit, Sin. That's it. Just like that. You're gonna make me come."

He holds me deep, tongue working that magic spot along the underside of my cock. Holy fuck—he's putting in work, and I'm unraveling with every second.

Hard to believe this is Will's first time going down on a man. You'd think with the way he expertly moves his tongue and works his throat that he's a bonafide cocksucker. The image of Will on his knees for anyone else blindsides me, and a fierce need to claim him surges hot through my veins.

I thrust with everything I have, chasing the tingles flowing through my bloodstream and landing straight between my legs.

"Gonna come, Sin."

I start to pull back, but his big hands clutch my ass and drive me deeper, burying me in his throat until his nose is pressed flush against me.

A string of curses leaves my lips in a rush as I release spurts of my cum into his mouth, coming and coming until the steam of the shower clouds everything around us.

His eyes widen as he struggles to swallow my load, full of desire. Aftershocks of my orgasm have me twitching against his tongue, and once I'm empty, I slowly slip myself out.

"Fuck, Sinclair. You sure you've never done that before?" I pant, tracing his lips with the head of my cock.

He licks the remnants of my release from the corners of his mouth before standing up and crushing his lips to mine. I taste myself on his tongue, my heart blooming with pride that he did something for the first time with me.

We kiss until the water turns cold, then rush through the rest of the shower, stealing kisses in between. An ease settles over us, something that's been happening more and more lately.

Will bares himself to me, giving me glimpses of something that I want more of. Every smile, laugh, and intimate moment spent with him has me envisioning a life I didn't see for myself. Sure, I've always wanted something akin to what my parents have. But I'm still early days in my career, and no one could truly understand the lifestyle this sport demands. Until Will. My teammate. An ex-rival, at that.

All this sneaking around can't last. Eventually, Will's gonna have to face reality and say the hard shit out loud. I'm not about to push him into something he's not ready for, but the lines keep blurring, and I'm not sure how much longer my head can fight what my heart already wants.

Safe to say, I'm down fucking bad.

Shit.

16

BROOKS

NOTHING COMPARES TO PLAYING in your home stadium. I'm one of the lucky ones who gets to play for the team in the city I was born and raised in. You can't beat the weather, the vibes, the overall ambience San Diego gives.

We had season tickets to the Rays games growing up. My earliest memories are here in this stadium, scarfing down dollar hot dogs and a half gallon of soda while Jade wore giant headphones to protect her ears from the roar of the crowd, and Mom and Dad cheered on their favorite players.

My eyes never left the catcher, though. Watching him call the plays and hold power in his position by having a vantage point of the entire field. Like he was a maestro leading an orchestra.

Dad always said it was my calling to be a catcher. I was meant to be low in the dirt, reading the field, seeing the whole game play out in front of me. There's a rhythm back there, a kind of control most people don't notice. Everyone watches the pitcher, but it's the catcher who sets the tempo, who keeps the game moving.

I love the grind of it—the bruises, the sore knees, the dirt caked on my gear. It's not pretty, but it's real. And I get to be the anchor, the one the team leans on without even realizing it. Some guys chase the spotlight. I'm fine in the shadows, calling the shots from behind the plate. That's where I belong.

Then I look out at the mound and see the man I can't take my mind—or eyes—off of these days. The sun beats down on us, beads of sweat falling down my temple under my mask. Will stands tall in the distance, shuffling the ball between his fingers as he uses his shoulder to swipe at his forehead.

We're up by three against Philadelphia, and Will has been playing fucking solid. Say what you want about the man, but over a decade in the league and he still plays as if he's fresh out of high school. Will Sinclair is a goddamn machine.

Philadelphia's Deacon Fraser steps up to the plate, tapping his cleats against the dirt with that cocky little routine he always does. On paper, he's average. Hits the ball about two times out of every ten at-bats this season. Not terrible, but nowhere near the slugger he thinks he is.

Crouching low behind home plate, I give Will a signal. I didn't win the all-star rookie award three years ago for nothing. I study these guys and know them like the back of my hand. If only Fraser could see the smirk from beneath my mask.

Fraser can't resist swinging when a pitch is high and tight near his chest. The numbers don't lie. Nearly a third of the time he'll chase that ball even when he shouldn't.

"You got this, Sin," I mutter under my breath, flashing for a fastball that'll fuck over Fraser. As Will gets into position, I flash him my *own signal*, biting back a grin.

Fastball, up and in. I want your dick.

Stoic as ever, Will pulls down the bill of his cap, digging his cleats into the dirt. He takes a deep breath before his lips slowly tilt into the sexiest smirk.

That one's for me.

He winds up, and within a second, the ball hits my mitt with a loud pop.

Strike.

The noise of the crowd falls away, and it's just me and Will on the field, eyes locked on each other like nothing else matters. I could be in the middle of a sand storm and I'd still find him. My heart flutters with these emotions, but I shake it off since I'm in the middle of a fucking game.

I flash another signal.

Pitch.

Pop.

Strike.

Rinse and repeat. Will strikes out Fraser and the crowd goes wild.

"Fuck yeah, Sin! Let's go, baby!" I shout as I jog up to the mound.

Clapping his shoulder, he brings his mitt to cover his mouth and leans in my ear. "You're gonna pay for that fucking signal, War," he rasps low, my body vibrating with the gravel in his voice.

I cover my mouth and tell him, "That's what I was hoping for, Pretty Boy."

Post-game press sucks ass. When Coach Hunter called me for media, I seriously debated running to my car and hauling ass straight to Will's place. But then he called for Sinclair as well, and now I'm sitting behind the press table with a mega-watt smile on my face next to Will.

We're sitting so close I can smell the fresh scent of his soap from his shower earlier, and all the dirty images I have of him are swirling around in my mind, completely ignoring the reporters asking questions about the game. I'm fully checked out to everyone else but him, and I'm counting down the minutes until I can get him alone.

Time drones on, and I'm close to nodding off when an incessant buzzing jolts my shoulders straight, coming from Will's pocket.

He pulls out his phone just enough to see the name *Jerry* flash on the screen. He ends the call, stuffing his phone back into his pocket when it vibrates not even two seconds after. We eye each other with trepidation, curious to why his agent is blowing up his phone.

"Last question," Coach announces, pointing at the reporter from the San Diego Tribune.

"Will," the reporter says, grabbing Will's attention away from his buzzing pocket.

Will clears his throat. "Yes?"

"It's known that you've been a bachelor throughout your years here in the league. While most players your age are already married and have young children, your single status is something the media has always held interest in."

Will's body stiffens from where he sits, and I can feel the tension rolling off his shoulders at this stupid fucking question.

I'm about to cut in and ask this guy what the hell his point is when he adds on, "Is your sexuality the reason you've kept your dating life so private—especially now that it's out that you're gay?"

Audible gasps and murmurs echo throughout the small conference room, and my mouth gapes so wide at the absurdity and unprofessionalism of this asshole. I turn to Will, whose face is white as a sheet, devoid of color.

His eyes glaze over, completely frozen in time as reporters shout for his attention and bright flashes from cameras go off in waves.

"We're getting the hell out of here," I murmur in Will's ear, grabbing him by the elbow and dragging him out of his seat.

Coach takes the brunt of the assault from reporters, doing his best to calm the crowd. He and I make eye contact, and he gives me a quick nod before Will and I slip through the exit door where we're met by security.

It's all a blur as security escorts us to the parking lot where Will's Range Rover is parked next to my car.

"Hand me your keys," I tell him once we're at his passenger side door.

He doesn't react or respond to me, body completely drained of emotion, and that has my heart stampeding like a pack of wild horses. I try again, louder this time.

"Will! Keys, baby. Please." I soften my voice, eyes pleading for him to hear me.

Finally, a sign of life as he digs for his car keys in his pocket and hands them over to me. I unlock the car and get him in, shutting the door with force, then jog toward the driver's side.

We're out of the stadium lot in less than a minute, flying down the street to get him home. Home with me. Home where it's safe.

My mind goes to overdrive, fixating on getting Will as far away from this bullshit as possible. Where the fuck did that reporter get that information? We've been discreet ever since we've gotten together. There's no way he would've known anything happened between us.

Guilt rips through me like a lightning bolt, burning me at the thought that I could've caused this pain I feel permeating from him. The bluetooth from his phone automatically connects to his car, and his father's name pops up on the dash like an ominous warning.

Jameson Sinclair's name flashes on the screen again and again. I silence each call, glancing at Will every time. His head's buried between his knees, hands clutching his skull like he can squeeze the noise out, like he wants the whole world to fall away.

I make all the familiar turns toward his beach house, hands gripping the wheel with white knuckles like my life depends on it.

Like *his life* depends on it.

17

WILLIAM

Behind Closed Doors

What was once hot water has turned freezing cold, causing goose-bumps to unleash over my skin. Drops of ice pelt the back of my head as I sit on my shower bench with my head in my hands. The need to cry presses behind my eyes, but the tears won't fall. I'm numb from the inside out.

What was I thinking being so careless—so reckless—when it came to hooking up with Brooks?

The truth is I wasn't thinking at all. At least not with my head—the correct one, that is.

Over the past decade I've been in the league, I've been meticulous when it comes to having women sign NDAs. If they weren't willing to sign one, I wasn't willing to touch them. End of story.

But when it comes to Brooks, I have a tendency to lose sight of my obligations, throwing caution to the wind.

And look where that got me.

I can't believe the woman we decided not to share in Milwaukee sold my story to the press.

Stupid. I'm so fucking *stupid.*

I'm not sure how long I've been in here, but I don't fight Brooks when he opens the glass door to my shower and turns off the water. He grabs a towel off the hook and wraps it around my shoulders, and I can't find it in me to be anything but despondent.

By the time I've dried off and thrown on a pair of boxer briefs, Brooks is nowhere to be found.

Left to my own devices, I sulk in my bed and do the one thing Brooks and Jerry, my agent, told me not to do.

I turn on my phone.

I'm immediately overwhelmed with the flood of notifications for tags in news articles, missed texts, and voicemails.

This was a bad idea. I should turn it back off, but I double down instead, clicking on a link I've been tagged in on social media that leads me to a well-known trashy gossip site that claims to be the one to break the story of my sexuality.

The headline reads: "MLB All-Star outed after being seen with a mystery partner."

Below the headline is a blurry photo of me kissing Brooks in the hallway of our hotel pressed up against the door of our room in Milwaukee.

The photo is grainy, yet it very clearly shows my face with my head thrown back as Brooks sucks on my neck, only showing the back of his head in the frame.

It's damning.

My reputation—my legacy on the game—will all go to shit because of this scandal. It will forever hang over my head; there's no doubt in my mind.

I drop my phone and pull at my damp hair.

Why the hell is this happening to me?

So what if I'm into Brooks? Hooking up with one man doesn't make me gay. I've been with dozens of women. I *like* women. I'm pretty sure that makes me bi-sexual. And even *that* isn't something I'm comfortable with being thrown around by the media.

My sex life is just that—*mine*. My sexuality is still something I'm coming to terms with; I didn't need some fucking reporter to blow up my entire world before I even knew what was going on.

This is such bullshit.

These vultures can't get away with this. I won't let them.

Shock is replaced by adrenaline, and suddenly I need to do something—anything—to combat the fury being outed has awakened within me. Before I can find an outlet, Brooks nudges my bedroom door open with a tray of food in his hands.

"What are you doing?" I question, noticing the steam rising from a bowl on the tray.

He shrugs nonchalantly, setting the tray on my bedside table and sitting on the edge of the bed. "I made my mom's avgolemono soup. You gotta eat something."

I look at Brooks with a mix of apprehension and unbridled anger that I know I have no right directing at him right now, though I can't help it.

When he blows on a spoonful of soup before bringing it to my lips, something snaps inside of me.

Swatting the spoon away from my lips, I hiss, "I don't want to fucking eat right now."

Brooks sets the bowl down and turns to face me with far more patience than I deserve. "I understand you're angry right now, but I'm just trying to help."

"Well stop trying to help. Because you *helping* is what got me here."

He takes a deep, resigned breath. "Look, I understand—"

"You understand?!" I cut him off, shaking my head. "No, you don't understand. You didn't just get outed in front of the whole world!" I shout, my chest heaving.

Brooks stays quiet, silently urging me to keep going—to get it all off my chest.

My chin trembles, and I hate the vulnerability written all over my face. "I'm not like you. I can't just go around and flaunt my relationships with men and women. I have a reputation to uphold, and now it's ruined."

His jaw feathers in frustration. "Since when did you ever care about that?"

My brows draw together from his question.

So he continues, "You of all people should know that your reputation doesn't mean shit. Your own father traded you."

"What the fuck does that mean?" I grit out.

Brooks' eyes soften just a bit. "It means you made a name for yourself outside of being St. Louis' star pitcher. We're your family now. We're here to protect you. I'm here to take care of you if you'd just let me."

"Take care of me? Can't you see this is your fault!" I shout, sitting up so I'm right in his face. "If it wasn't for you messing with my head, I would've had that woman sign an NDA like I have for every fucking hookup I've had over the last decade."

Brooks edges closer. "It's not just my fault. Sure, I didn't have my head about me either, but look where that night got us. It brought us here," he rasps, his tone full of pleading. "This will pass. I know right now it doesn't feel like it, but it will. And you have me and your teammates to lean on—we're all here for you."

Shaking my head, I lower my voice in resignation. "You can't speak for them. They probably all think I'm a dick for the way I treated them when I first got here."

"I'm not speaking for them. If you'd open the team group chat, you'd know they're all blowing up your phone with messages of support."

"I'll look later. I've had enough of my phone for the time being," I grumble, sitting back against my headboard with my arms across my chest.

Brooks sits up and nudges me with his knee. "Scoot over. If you're gonna sit here and sulk, I might as well commiserate with you."

I hesitate a moment before moving over to make room.

We sit in silence, but the weight of his stare is heavy.

"You can go home—you don't need to sit here and babysit me."

That earns me a scoff. "I'm not babysitting you. I care about you, and this is me showing up for you."

"Well maybe you shouldn't," I tell him before I can think better of it.

He tenses beside me. "Why?"

"Because it's bad enough what they're all saying about me. But if they find out you're my 'mystery man,' it'll only fan the flames until our whole season goes up in smoke."

"Fuck everyone else," he's quick to retort.

"God, Warren. That's not how life works. We can't just live our lives holding up a big metaphorical middle finger to the world, especially not when we're in the public eye," I admonish.

"Then we'll keep it a secret, keep everything behind closed doors."

"Yeah? And how do you suggest we do that?"

"Here. At your place. Away from the press and all the bullshit. We can still do this on your terms. My only condition: I'm not going anywhere. So you can push me away, yell at me, call me every name in the book, but I'm. Not. Fucking. Leaving."

I dig the heels of my hands into my eye sockets, shaking my head back and forth with a mix of frustration and gratitude at his willingness to stay. But I'm too fucked in my head to see the light at the end of the tunnel right now.

All I see is a damning headline. A ruined reputation. A mockery with my name all over it.

"I can't do this with you right now, War."

"Will, please—"

"Just give me some space." I blow out a tired breath. "Alright?"

Brooks' eyes bore into mine, pleading with a flash of hurt. A small part of me hates that I put that look on his face, but I need him to leave before I make things worse.

He gives me a small nod, leaning in to press a gentle kiss on the corner of my mouth. Without a word, he slips out of my bed.

With the soft click of my door shutting behind him, I let myself break.

18

WILLIAM

Use Me

My body naturally wakes me before the sun comes up. You'd think I drank an entire handle of liquor before bed with the splitting headache I have. I'm completely naked, not bothering to have even put on a pair of briefs before I passed out.

With one eye open, my room is dark and empty, only a sliver of blue light streaming in from my window. Instinctively, I reach beside me, only to be met with cold sheets.

My heart sinks the minute Brooks enters my head. Since we've been roommates on the road, I've gotten used to his warmth on my skin, his breath on my neck, his lips . . . all over me first thing in the morning.

But I fucked that all to hell last night when I all but kicked him out of my house because I couldn't get a handle on my shit.

Rolling onto my back, I look up at the ceiling and rub a fist over my chest where it aches from how I treated him. Shifting my gaze to the side table, I see the soup he brought me last night, cold and untouched.

"Fuck," I mutter, tossing the blanket off me before throwing on only a pair of clean briefs and athletic shorts.

I need to run this off and think of how I'm going to apologize to him. In the clear light of day, I realize I was too harsh.

From an early age, I've had to look out for myself. I poured myself cereal every morning, regardless of the breakfast spread our home chef made every day. I got myself to baseball practice an hour before everyone else to put in extra work and escape from the loneliness of a big, empty house. My parents would pawn me off with a driver to most of my tournaments, and when I'd look up in the stands, there was no one there for me.

I quickly learned I'm the only person I could ever truly rely on.

However, as I make my way down the stairs, I recognize that might not be the case.

Standing frozen on the bottom step, I take in Brooks lying on my sofa, limbs splayed in a way I know can't be comfortable. He's shirtless, his broad chest rising and falling in a rhythm I've become accustomed to.

He stayed.

Peace replaces the uncertainty and doubt that consumed me in the darkness of the night. Within a few quiet strides, I kneel at the edge of the couch, close enough to hear Brooks' soft breathing.

I can't help but give into my need to touch him. Reaching out, I gently brush his hair off of his forehead, then lean in to place a kiss on his lips.

He stirs, eyelids fluttering open. It takes him a moment to register where he is, but when his gaze focuses on mine, a sleepy smile breaks across his face.

"Hey," he rasps, stretching his arms above his head.

"Hi." I smile back. "You're still here."

Brooks threads his fingers through my hair, pulling me closer to him. "I told you I wasn't going anywhere," he whispers against my skin.

"But I was an asshole to you."

"Nothing new to me, Sinclair," he points out, breaking the tension with the smirk that's become my weakness.

"Thank you," I murmur.

A lone tear slips free as the realization sinks in, trailing down my cheek until Brooks catches it with the pad of his thumb. I watch with hooded eyes as he brings his thumb to his mouth and sucks my tears.

There's an intensity in our gazes, immediately heating up the room a hundred degrees. This man has me unraveling, stealing the breath from me not only from his words but from his actions.

No one would've stayed after the way I treated him. He's proven to be a man of his word despite the ugliness I threw his way. Each hit I gave, he took with grace.

I don't deserve the kindness he's showing me, but with the way he looks at me like I'm the center of his universe, I might believe that I *do* deserve better.

For the first time in far too long, I don't feel alone.

"You don't need to thank me, Will. Even when you push me away, I'm going to prove to you I'm not going anywhere."

His sincerity and fierce need to protect me have me taken aback. I'm overcome with gratitude mixed with an insatiable desire to devour him.

"Good. You're starting to grow on me," I say with a small smile.

The energy shifts into something darker between us, and a teasing grin pulls the corners of Brooks' mouth. He whispers low into my ear, "You're lucky I'm so stubborn."

Brooks nips my earlobe, eliciting shivers down my neck. I groan when he licks the shell of my ear, his breath against my skin creating goosebumps in its wake. My cock hardens, tenting my shorts.

"You're doing it again," I pant against his cheek.

"What?" he asks, feigning innocence.

"Driving me crazy, baby."

I desperately need to feel his skin on mine, and when he runs his calloused fingertips down my abs, something inside me snaps.

"Upstairs. Now," I growl as I practically drag him up the steps back to my bedroom.

Pushing him on the bed, I crawl to him and claim his lips. We kiss like our lives depend on it. Nipping, biting, sucking, and fucking each other's mouths with reckless abandon.

I could get lost in him as we grind our erections together, desperately seeking friction. Only the thin fabric of my shorts and his briefs separate us, and with the way we move against one another, there's nothing we want more than our skin to touch.

In one swift movement, Brooks rolls on top of me, his gaze locked onto mine. There's a sort of reverence in his eyes as he whispers against my lips, "Use me, Will. Take back your control."

My chest heaves as every fiber of my being craves to take back even an ounce of the control that was stolen from me. He's giving me a gift that I can't refuse. It's permission. Something I've been longing for.

"If I take it back, there's only one thing I want."

His breath stutters before replying, "Yeah? And what is it that you want? Say it."

"To claim you. Every part of you."

"And how do you intend to do that, Sin?"

"I'm going to fuck you, War."

Hovering above me, he sinks his teeth into his plush bottom lip, rolling his hips over mine. "What are you waiting for?"

Without another word, I flip him over on his back again and kneel above his thighs.

"Strip. Then get on all fours."

A slow smile spreads across his face.

Brooks props himself up on his elbows without breaking eye contact and scoots back, taking his time as he slowly works his hands into the waistband of his briefs.

Fucking tease.

With barely restrained desire, my nostrils flare as I ball my hands into fists to prevent me from doing it for him.

Narrowing my gaze, I shoot him a look that says *Oh, you wanna play? Game on.*

"Turn over," I command, and my dick twitches when Brooks obeys, getting on all fours like I told him to earlier.

I swallow hard past the vulnerability of this moment—the first time I fuck him.

We've gotten each other off countless times with our hands and mouths, and we're no strangers at this point to ass play. Brooks has coached me through it each time, but I want this to be different. I need to be in control.

Reaching across to my bedside table, I open the drawer and pull out a bottle of lube but hesitate when I see the condoms. We're both regularly tested, and we haven't hooked up with anyone else, so there's really no need.

Brooks must read my mind because he rasps, "Take me bare."

"You sure?" I question.

"What, are you scared because I'm not on the pill?" he taunts.

"You're such a fucking brat."

He tries but fails to bite back a menacing smile. "I am. You should probably punish me for it."

"You'd like that, wouldn't you?"

Brooks rocks back to sit on his heels, but my answering tut of disapproval stops him.

With only the lube in hand, I shift back and push down on his neck. "Did I say you could move?"

"No," he replies breathlessly.

I situate myself behind him and pause as I take him in. He's on all fours with his legs spread as I kneel between them. With his face pressed against the mattress, he looks up over his shoulder at me, and I marvel at the way his eyes are half-mast, swimming with seduction. Overcome by the sudden urge to kiss him, I bend down to take his mouth, sucking his bottom lip into mine before biting down on it. His answering groan has my dick twitching against his ass, reminding us both where this is going.

As I sit back, I bite down hard on his shoulder as a punishment for disobeying me.

"Ah, motherfucker! That hurt," Brooks hisses, causing me to chuckle.

"Want me to kiss it better, or do you want me to do something else?" I ask as I grab the bottle of lube off the bed.

Brooks follows my hand and shakes his head. "No. You can make it up to me by getting my ass nice and ready for you."

I open the bottle and squeeze it over his crack, watching the way the lube trails down his ass. My cock throbs thinking about what it'll look like when I finish inside him and it's my cum seeping out.

As I work the lube in, I slowly push one finger past the tight ring of muscle, eliciting a groan of approval from Brooks. And when I add a second finger, his back arches to give me better access.

Pulling my fingers from him before he can find any sort of relief, I circle his hole at a torturous rate, teasing him as I slowly work my cock up and down.

Brooks lets out a growl of frustration. "Would you fuck me already?"

I let out a menacing chuckle. "I'll fuck you when I want to fuck you."

"But I've waited for this for so long."

"I don't know, doesn't sound like you want it enough."

"I do."

Slapping his cheek with my dick, I hiss, "Beg me to fuck you."

"What?"

"Do you want me or not?"

He whimpers, writhing beneath my touch.

"Do you?"

Nodding desperately, he pushes back against me, but I *tsk*.

"Then beg for my cock, baby."

He's silent, so I decide to really amp up the torture. Nudging his asshole with just the tip of my dick, I line myself up like I'll fuck him, but when he rocks his hips back again, I pull away.

"Beg."

A frustrated whine escapes him. "Please, Will. Please fuck me. I'll do anything you want."

His compliance has me nearly coming undone right then and there. I squirt a handful of lube into my palm and work it over my length. Unwilling to wait a second longer, I toss the bottle aside and prod the head of my cock inside his ass, slowly giving him an inch.

"*Fuck!*" I growl, marveling at the snug feel of him.

As I press my hips forward, I have to grip his hips tightly to ground myself. I've never felt so unsure of myself while having sex with someone. Well, that's not entirely true. I probably felt something similar to this when I lost my virginity. And I suppose in some way, I'm cashing in my v-card right now.

Bringing one leg up so I'm kneeling on one knee, I use the new position as leverage to piston my hips deeper until I finally bottom out.

"Oh, shit," Brooks mewls. "You've got the biggest fucking cock."

I freeze, unwilling to move while also allowing Brooks time to adjust.

When he pulls his hips forward and slams them back against me, I take that as my queue to move again.

The room fills with sounds of our harmonized groans of pleasure and the slapping of our skin.

Looking down, I watch with rapt fascination as he sucks me in. "You're taking me so well, baby. I can't stop looking at the way your ass is suffocating my cock."

Shifting his legs wider, he eagerly takes everything I'm giving to him. "I'm not lying when I say literally no one else would be able to take you like this, Sin."

"Yeah? Is that because this ass was made for me, War?" I question, gripping his hips so tightly I know I'll leave bruises. The thought of marking him turns me feral.

"It was," he admits, panting for breath.

"It was, wasn't it. You wanna know why? Because it's mine. *You're mine.*"

Reaching around his waist, I grip his length in my hand and squeeze. My hand is still wet with the lube I used on myself, so when I begin pumping my fist up and down his shaft, there's no uncomfortable friction, just pure pleasure. Throwing his head back, he groans in ecstasy.

I grind my hips frantically, only halting my movements when I get so deep we simultaneously moan. Leaning forward, I kiss his shoulder over the bite mark I left earlier and grit out, "God, you feel so fucking good. Should've fucked your ass weeks ago."

"Think of all we've been missing." He hums his heady reply.

Sitting back on my heels, I tell him, "Take over for me, baby. Fist your cock and come all over the sheets while I come in your ass."

He whimpers, and the sound goes straight to my cock, making it throb in anticipation.

"I'm gonna make a mess out of you."

"Please," he begs in eager agreement. "I'm so close. Just like that. Come with me, Sin."

That's all it takes for me to unravel alongside him. "Fuck, holy fuck!"

As I come inside of him, I feel his hips jolt with his release as black dots spot my vision.

I curl over him, completely spent and breathless from our mutual release. The biggest smile spreads over my face because that was the hottest fucking thing I've ever done.

"How long until we can do that again?" I ask in a dazed tone.

Brooks breathes out a tired laugh. "Let's take a shower first."

"Can I fuck you in there?"

"Who'd have thought my ass would turn you into a sex addict?"

"It's a great ass," I retort.

"So I've been told."

Growling in disapproval, I sit back and swat his ass. "Keep running your mouth and you're gonna pay for it later," I warn.

"I'm counting on it," he tosses back with a sexy smirk.

Slipping out of him, we both groan at the loss of me being inside. I stare with complete primal hunger as my cum slowly leaks out, leaving a thick white trail dripping down to his balls.

I lean back and admire my work. "Damn, would you look at that? Maybe I should just leave you leaking of me all day long," I muse.

Brooks drops to his stomach in a fit of laughter. "Who knew sex was all we needed to do for you to say more than two words to me? You're fucking funny in your post-nut bliss."

Rolling onto his back, he laces his fingers behind his head. Brooks looks up at me with a hazy gaze, almost like his eyes are smiling at me.

Leaning over him, I give him a quick kiss, but when I pull back, he's still got the same look in his eyes. "Why are you looking at me like that?"

"Like what?"

"Like you've got stars in your eyes—"

"They're *moony eyes*," he cuts me off, grinning.

"What the hell does that mean?"

Brooks chuckles, digging his heels into my ass so all my weight lands on top of him. "Trust me, it's a good thing."

"As long as you don't give anyone else those eyes," I whisper against his mouth.

"Only for you, Pretty Boy."

19

BROOKS

So Far Gone

WE CHASE OUR BREATHS, panting, every ounce of energy wrung from our bodies. My heart slams against my ribs, sweat dripping between my pecs and trailing down past my navel.

Will grunts, the steady thuds matching mine, spurring me to push harder. Each strained breath, each burn in my muscles, brings me closer to collapse, legs threatening to give out.

"Ah, fuck!" Will shouts.

"Fuck you!" I fire back, my foot edging just past his before we both collapse onto the sand, groaning through our laughter.

What was meant to be a low-key morning jog spiraled into a full-on beach race, leaving us sprawled out on the shoreline, chests heaving and grins plastered across our faces.

A perk of having my man own a sick beach house is private access to his little slice of paradise. No paparazzi or unwanted eyes. No media or anyone who doesn't belong in our orbit.

Ever since that desperate-for-attention fan outed Will, we've taken full advantage of the privacy his home offers and have been laying low. A silver lining to this whole mess is that it hit right before the All-Star break.

The Rays gave Will extra leave on top of that, knowing the media frenzy would be impossible to juggle. His agent, Jerry, has been working double overtime to keep reporters off his back. The photos that leaked on that trashy gossip site only showed the back of my head.

The "mystery man" Will's swapping spit with is still unknown to the public eye. I insisted on making my identity known to take some heat off Will, but he's drawn a firm line in the sand on the matter, telling me it won't do the situation any good.

I hate to see him hurting. He's doing a damn good job of hiding it now, but I know deep down he's struggling. So, I offer him what I can to distract him—sex and more sex.

"You cheated," Will pants, rolling his head toward me.

"God, you're such a sore loser, Sin. Admit it. You're just an old man. So suck it."

"Suck this," he fires back with a smirk, palming himself through his shorts.

"You'd like that, wouldn't you?"

Our laughter floats effortlessly from us, something that's been easy lately—despite the circus happening outside our bubble.

The bubble pops when Will's watch rings, his eyes rolling when Jerry's name flashes across the screen. He hits ignore.

"You just gonna ignore every call you get?" I ask, sitting up in the sand.

Will sits up with me, dusting the sand off his hands against his shorts. The sound of the ocean waves fills the silence, and I watch as Will squints toward the open water like he's contemplating whether or not to swim out as deep as he can and never come back.

"Listen, Sinclair," I start, slowly linking our fingers together. "You know I'll happily live in this reality where no one but you and I exist. But sooner or later, we gotta get back out there. We can't hide forever."

He meets my gaze with a look of peace I haven't seen in a while. A soft smile grazes his mouth as he gives my hand a squeeze before standing to brush the sand off his bottom.

He helps me up, then pulls me in until we're chest to chest. I don't expect the soft kiss he presses to my lips, but it makes my stomach flip anyway. Like a runaway train, Will Sinclair has me off the goddamn rails with just one kiss.

It's scary how much power he holds over me, no matter how much I downplay it. It's easier to think I can be there for him as his friend with benefits than it is to think that something deeper is happening between us.

Will's sexuality is a fragile thing—one I'm not willing to break.

"This weekend is my family's annual gala. Jerry's probably blowing me up because my dad's definitely hounding him for my lack of communication," Will grumbles.

"So fuck it, then. Don't go. Your dad doesn't control your life. You're a grown man, and you don't owe him shit."

His laugh is empty, and he shakes his head like I've just said the most incredulous thing. "I have to go. It's important not just to my family, but to me."

"Okay?" I drag out the word, trying not to get lost in his scent that's causing my mind to wander to less innocent things. Will's opening up to me, and all I can think about is how badly I want to lick the sweat gleaming off his chest. *Jesus.* "Care to elaborate?"

There's a sadness in his eyes, his face falling just slightly. It's enough for me to notice the shift in the air, a heaviness suddenly sitting between us.

"Remember how I mentioned my sister?"

I nod.

"The gala is in honor of her. O-of her life."

My throat thickens with emotion. Will doesn't have to say it out loud for me to read between the lines. I can feel his grief from here, along with the other swirl of emotions he's been battling since his world came to an implosion.

"When?" I simply ask.

"She was eleven. Leukemia. I was thirteen, and she was my whole world. The day she died, a part of me died with her. My family hasn't been the same since."

Instantly, I think of Jade. My little sister who will forever hold the title of best friend. The one sibling I have who I'd burn the whole world down for. If she were to ever be . . . fuck. I can't even think of it.

My arms circle Will's waist, pulling him flush to me. Resting my head in the crook of his neck, I hold him there and let every apology and sympathy I have for his loss seep out of me that words can't do justice.

When I feel drops of liquid fall onto my shoulder, I squeeze him tighter.

I don't know how long we stand there on the beach holding each other. Salt in the air wafts around us like a comforting blanket, and the heat of the sun reminds us we're alive and not alone.

Will releases me, our foreheads pressed together. "Tell me more about her," I whisper, our eyes closed.

"I'd love to. But first—" He leans in and claims my lips one more time, swiping his tongue once inside my mouth like a tease. Our eyes open at the same time, a little spark shining in his again. "Can you make some breakfast? I'm starving."

"Hmm, but you lost. It's only fair you cook," I tease as I nip his bottom lip.

"Is that what you really want? Toast burnt to hockey pucks and rubbery eggs?"

My shoulders shudder thinking about Will's shitty cooking skills. He's got time. I'll get him there.

"Fine. But you owe me."

Without another word, Will Sinclair sinks to his knees in the sand, taking my shorts down with him.

"Did you see me on that last set? I looked like a pro," Mateo gloats, his smile just as blinding as the sun's reflection off the water.

We both straddle our boards, floating in between waves. Outside of baseball, surfing has been an escape since I was a kid. My dad was an avid surfer and taught me as soon as I was strong enough to paddle out on my own.

We didn't live walking distance to the beach, having had to drive almost half an hour toward the coast, but damn, I loved those mornings. Boards strapped to the top of my dad's beat up station wagon, windows down with my head sticking out the entire way like a dog until the scent of saltwater hit my nose.

Taking a deep inhale, I run my fingers through my soaked hair. "You're getting better, I'll give you that."

"I had a good teacher. If you didn't play baseball, I could see you being a surf instructor."

I laugh, shaking my head at the nonsense of it. "Nah, man. Baseball is my first love. I love the water, but nothing compares to the game."

"You got that right, *papi*. I'd rather smell dirt than ocean water," Mateo muses.

"Ha. That's for sure."

We both stare out into the open water, looking for the hint of a swell coming. It's calm out there with no sign of another set coming through. "But it's still pretty fucking beautiful out here. I mean, shit. Look at that," I say, pointing at the sun dipping lower into the horizon.

We float in silence as the sky shifts from blue to orange. Mateo and I haven't always been this friendly. Once upon a time, he and I couldn't stand to be within five feet from each other. We still give each other constant shit and square up in a heated argument or two, but over the years, we've formed a friendship I've come to appreciate.

It helps that Mateo is bisexual like me. I never had to hide my sexuality with him, and although we butt heads more often than not, he's never judged me for my desires. He gets it. We are two openly queer, professional ball players in a league that can be stuck in their old ways.

And even though we've both made headlines in the tabloids for our "lifestyle," we've never crossed the line. We've shared many women—and men—in the past, but I've never even laid my lips on the guy.

I could say it's because we're teammates and we didn't want to blur the lines, but that's far from the truth. Truth is, Mateo and I have as much chemistry as a wet match and a brick wall.

On the field? We're in sync. I can read him like a book. In the bedroom? Nada. Zilch. *Zero.*

"How's Sinclair doing?"

"He's alright. Good days and bad days." I keep things vague because I don't know how Will would feel if I were to air out his business to someone he doesn't fully trust.

Yeah, we're all teammates, but as pretty as Sinclair is—he's skittish.

"You can do better than that. I know you like him, War. Don't bullshit me."

Mateo whips his hand against the water, splashing me in the face. I sputter, *maturely* splashing him back. We go back and forth a few times before we're both laughing and over it.

"Alright, chill the fuck out. I like him, okay? A lot. He's . . . I don't know. He's just—"

"Different?" Mateo tacks on.

I nod as my mouth wants to twitch into a smile. "I don't know, man. It just sort of happened. And now after all this shit with him being outed and his reputation on the line—I just want to be there for him. Make it all go away, you know?"

Mateo makes a low whistle, shaking his head with a grin. "No, I don't know. But I hope I do some day, *papi*. Happiness looks good on you."

"Thanks," I mutter under my breath, cheeks heating under the weight of his compliment.

Damn. That's the thing. I am happy. Even if I'm only getting pieces of Will, it's more than nothing. Even if he tells me over and over "I'm not gay," I have to trust deep down he feels something *more* for me.

Tell that to the way he holds me after we have sex. Or the way he belly laughs at my stupid ass jokes. Or how he kisses me after every meal I cook for him, gratitude pouring out of his heart.

That's something, right?

Thoughts like this further prove how far gone I am for Will Sinclair. It proves how far I'm willing to go for a hint of a smile, so long as that smile is for no one else but me.

An idea strikes at the forefront of my mind so quickly I don't realize I'm smiling until Mateo bumps his board with mine.

"What's with the face, War?"

"I just thought of something epic, but I need your help."

20

WILLIAM

Patience Is A Virtue

From my view on the balcony, I watch waves crash the shore, the rhythm steadying my heart rate as I contemplate whether or not I want to press the call button next to my dad's name.

He's been calling me incessantly since the news broke under the guise of wanting to discuss the gala at the end of this week. Each time I've rejected his call, refusing to talk to him in order to keep the fraction of peace being here in this bubble with Brooks has given me.

But like everything in life, all good things must come to an end. The respite I've found while laying low at my house with him is about to expire. I'll soon need to face reality when I attend the gala, and unfortunately that means it's time to face my father too.

Before I can contemplate it further, I press call and take a deep, calming breath.

Jameson Sinclair doesn't answer the phone with the typical hello—no, because he once told me greetings are a waste of time and it's best to get straight to the point.

Instead he says, "Glad you finally found time to call me back."

"Hello to you too, Dad," I retort, just to ruffle his feathers a bit.

"Thought you'd be easier to get a hold of since you've got time off right now." I'm not quite sure what to make of his tone. I thought he'd be disappointed if not borderline hostile when I spoke to him, especially after ignoring his calls for days. Instead, he sounds . . . worried? My suspicions peak when he asks, "How are you, William?"

I let out a sigh of exasperation. "Dad, just cut to the chase. I know you don't really care how I'm doing."

"How could you say that?"

Instead of trauma dumping all of the ways he's lacked as a father in the years since Abigail died, I grit out, "Let's just get this over with."

"Were the dozens of calls to you not proof enough that I care?"

"If you think calling me nonstop during one of the shittiest times in my life and career is you showing up for me, then you don't know me at all."

"I know you better than you think."

"You've had a funny way of showing it over the past twenty years."

There's a pause on the line, tension pulled taut without us even needing to be face-to-face. The stillness between us brews almost to the point of discomfort. My father's the first to break the silence, letting out a sigh of resignation on the other end. "Let me try this again. Are you okay?"

My throat swells at the sincerity in his question, the unexpected softness in his tone. "I've been taking some time for myself, trying to come to terms with what was reported while also staying out of the public eye."

"I can understand that, and I'm glad to hear San Diego is doing right by you and giving you extra time off if you need it."

I can't hold back my scoff at that. "Right. Because you care so much about my baseball career."

Yeah, I'm laying it on a little thick. My mother always told me grudges are a waste of perfect happiness. I have to agree with her, but when it comes to my dad, all bets are off. He tends to bring out the worst in me.

"I do. I care an awful lot about the one and only thing that has ever brought you any joy. Though, I'll admit it became more of an obsession at some point along the way."

Here it is. Time to have the conversation we've been dancing around for months.

"Oh yeah? Then why did you trade me?"

He's silent on the other end of the line for a few moments before finally answering, "I'm not a perfect father. I know that, and I never claimed to be. I traded you because I care about your individual future and successes more than my own team's."

I draw my brows together in confusion. "What does that even mean?"

"I saw how driven you were almost to the point of it being a detriment to your health. If you would've stayed home in St. Louis, it wouldn't have been long until you burned out."

As much as I hate to admit it, he's right. St. Louis was like living in a constant state of grief, memories of Abigail lingering in every corner of my life from my parents' home to the stadium I played at to her favorite ice cream shop down the road from where I practiced.

I could never escape the ache that lived deep in my chest—a hole that was left when my baby sister died. A hole made bigger with the broken state of my family and the distance my father put between us.

"Do you know what your record was on the road versus at home in all the years you played here?" he asks, breaking me from my thought spiral.

"No."

"Out of the nearly 250 games you played during your tenure here, you played and started about half of those on the road. You started for thirty team wins at home. On the road, you started for ninety wins."

"That's public information. A simple internet search could have anyone spewing those facts back to me."

I think I hear a whisper of a laugh, and I can imagine my father smirking on the line. He always did appreciate my talking back to him.

".523 batting average. Thirty-two RBIs. Forty-five strikeouts," he lists off without hesitation.

"What?"

"Your 13U stats. Information *not* found on the internet."

Something inside me breaks, hearing my father tell me my old stats from when I was a kid. I remember that summer. It was the worst of my life, only a few months after Abigail passed. Every game, I played for her.

Still do.

My stomach sinks and my mind fills with questions. "Okay, fine. Why didn't you talk to me earlier on if my game was suffering in St. Louis? Why did you trade me without a word?"

"It was for selfish reasons that your mother and I kept you in St. Louis for so long. We wanted you close. Your mother almost left me over the trade until I explained to her my reasons for doing so were in your best interest."

"And what—I wasn't worth having a conversation with?" My voice trembles.

He clears his throat. "No, it's not that. I suppose I thought you'd have an easier time moving on and playing the game you're capable of if you were pissed off at me instead."

"That rationale is so fucked," I hiss before I can think better of it.

"It was a cowardly move on my part."

His words give me pause. Throughout the last twenty years, he's never admitted to any wrong doing or apologized for much of anything. So why the sudden shift? Last time he was sentimental like this, he was telling us Abigail only had a short time left to live. Fuck, is someone sick? Is it Mom? Dawson? Shit, is it my dad and he's calling now to make some sort of final amends?

Panic seizes my chest but I manage to ask, "How is Mom doing through all this?"

"She's fine. She misses you. I mi—" He stops short. He sniffs before continuing. "When you come home for the gala, do you think you could take a few days and stay here with us since you've got the time off?"

Hesitation swarms my chest. "I'm not so sure that's a good idea. I-uh—"

I pause, scratching the back of my neck before squeezing my eyes shut and say, "I'm bringing someone."

"A date?"

"Yes. Well, at least I hope so."

"And is that someone the mystery person you were photographed with?"

I swallow down a lump in my throat. "It is."

"Is it serious?"

I consider my answer. Is it serious? Shit, I'm not sure how to answer that. Brooks and I haven't exactly put a label on anything we're doing. He hasn't left my side since the disastrous post-game interview until just an hour ago. And I can't deny I miss him. I wish he was here right now by my side while I'm having this conversation with my dad.

"It has the potential to be something serious."

"Well, that's good to hear. I'm excited to meet him."

Pulling my phone away from my ear, I look down at it to check my service because I had to have just heard him wrong. Did he just say *him*?

Did he just admit he's excited to meet the man I plan to bring as my date? Did he really just skirt over the fact that I was outed by national news outlets earlier this week and now I'll be potentially adding fuel to the fire by bringing a man as my date.

"He's my teammate," I admit.

"That makes it easier on the two of you while you're on the road to maintain a relationship. I know the intense travel schedule causes strain on some players' relationships."

Is he fucking with me right now?

"Aren't you going to ask who he is?"

"If I were to hedge a guess, I'd say Brooks Warren based on how he reacted when you threw your perfect game."

I smile to myself. "Wow, okay. So maybe we weren't as subtle as we thought."

"Nothing gets past me." He hums. "William, what I really want to see is you at your happiest. If that means you find your happiness with a man, so be it."

"But that isn't how you raised us growing up. Are you okay with having a son who is bisexual?"

Damn, that's the first time I've admitted I'm queer out loud. It came out easier than I thought it would, flowing from me with a confidence I didn't know existed.

Sometime during these past few days, I came to the realization that Brooks isn't my damnation.

Maybe he's become my salvation—helping me come to terms with who I really am.

"If it makes you happy to be with both men and women, I will make it a priority to educate myself and get up to speed so your mother and I can best support you."

My eyes well with tears—I don't think I fully grasped what it would mean to me to have his support and acceptance. It's all I ever wanted.

"Dad, I really appreciate that. It means more to me than you know."

Inside the house, I hear the security alarm beep, signaling the front door opening. The only person with the code to the house is Brooks, and the realization has my chest swelling with a foreign feeling.

"I hate to end the call early, but I've got to go. Can we talk before the gala, maybe?"

"Sure, Son. I'll see you then. Please tell Brooks he's welcome to stay at the house with you if you want."

I clear my throat. "I, uh, I'll let him know."

As the call ends, I set my phone down on the balcony ledge and hang my head in my hands. Squeezing my eyes shut, I blow out a breath I didn't realize I was holding as I run my fingers through my hair.

My father wants me to be happy. He's willing to accept me being with a man if it means I'm happy. And while my world has felt like it was falling apart around me, here in this house with Brooks over the past several days, I can't deny he's made me just that—happy and content beyond what I thought I was capable of feeling.

Brooks makes me feel cared for—fuck, adored even. I've leaned on him and opened up to him more than I have anyone else. I told him about Abigail and how my family has struggled since we lost her. I've shared my fears about what comes next and how I don't know who I'll be beyond baseball. Though those fears are slowly subsiding when I think about what it might be like to have someone to share my life with, not to be alone when that time comes. And that weird fluttering ache appears in my chest again when I think of the possibility of it being Brooks beside me when that time comes.

What would that be like? Would we spend our off season soaking up time here on the beach, or would we travel together? Does Brooks want something serious? Marriage? A family? Does he envision himself as a dad someday? Do I seriously want those things?

I could see us building a life together, but I'm not sure what to make of these feelings. I need time to sort through them. Time to ask him what he wants. Before we can do that, I need to ask him something else a bit more pressing.

The patio door slides open behind me, and within moments, strong arms wrap around my waist, Brooks' chest presses against my back, and his lips brush against the crook of my neck.

"Missed you," I murmur so quietly I'd think he missed it if it weren't for the stillness that takes over his body as my words sink in.

I clasp my fingers in his and turn in his arms to face him.

He looks at me with eyes full of incredulity. "You missed me?" he questions, his mouth turning up at the corners.

Nodding my response, I bite down on my bottom lip to stop myself from blurting out something I'm not sure we're ready for.

Giving myself time to think over what I'm about to ask, I bring him in for a kiss that is meant to be tender, but I quickly get caught up in the feel of his soft lips on mine. The pads of my fingers trail over the days-old scruff lining his jaw as one of his hands finds purchase at the nape of my neck, with the other grasping my lower back to pull me impossibly closer.

He lets out a groan when I lower my hand to grip around his throat, the sound going straight to my already thickening length. The feel of his fingers threading through my hair and tugging while his others simultaneously dig into my back so hard I pray he'll leave marks is driving me wild with lust and need for him. God, because only he can make me crazy.

Without breaking our kiss, I push him back against the glass door and thrust my hips into his, reveling in the way his bulge brushes against mine.

Moving my lips from his, I kiss a trail down his jaw and suck his neck before clamping down on his collarbone.

"Fuck, Will. I want you." He trails his hand down my bare chest, but I grab hold of it before he can dip it beneath the waistband of my athletic shorts.

Chest heaving against his, my nipples harden as they brush against the fabric of his shirt. "I want you too. But first, I need to ask you something."

He chuckles. "Okay, well, make it quick."

I stare into his eyes with conviction, but I'm not sure Brooks knows what to make of that because he whispers, "Is everything okay?"

Clearing my throat of the nerves clogging it, I tell him, "Yeah, everything is good. I just, uh, well I wanted to ask if you'd come to Abigail's gala with me?"

His gaze rakes over my face for so long I take a weighted breath in anticipation of his rejection.

"Of course. If you want me to come, I'll be there to support you in any way I can."

My brows crease. "No. Shit. I don't think I said that right. I want you to come *with* me."

"With you?" A smile teases the corners of his mouth.

I lick my lips, and on an exhale I clarify, "As my date."

His teasing smile turns radiant. Fuck, the happiness displayed on his face right now is magnificent. I have the sudden urge to do everything in my power to keep it there.

"Are you sure you're ready to make things public?" he questions, and my stomach churns with anxiety thinking about what the headlines will say about us. I quickly shove it down, not letting it get the best of me this time.

"Are you?" I echo back. "I just got off the phone with my dad. We had a good conversation."

"Really?" He does a poor job of tamping back his surprise.

"Yeah. I came out to him. He was . . . shockingly supportive. It really threw me for a fucking loop at first. I'm still trying to wrap my head around it. But it's a good start."

Brooks holds me closer, squeezing his arms tight around my middle. His happiness for me is radiant, rolling off of him and straight into my soul. It feels fucking good.

I pull back slightly, holding his eyes with mine. "And he said he's excited to meet you. If you're ready?"

"I'd love nothing more than to be able to hold your hand in public. To be able to kiss you whenever I want. But it's not just about me. Is that what you want?"

Is it? A swell of warmth spreads from my chest to my stomach when I think about being able to openly hold each other and show our affection in public. It's terrifying, but imagining Brooks on my arm makes this whole thing a lot less scary. He makes me believe it's something I can do.

And if not for him, I'll do it for me.

"Stepping outside of our bubble obviously leaves us vulnerable to criticism from others, but you've proved to me over the past several days that I need to stop worrying about what others think and put my wants and needs first and forget about the noise." I grin, brushing my nose against his. "So yeah, that's what I want. To be able to be with you out in the open. *Exclusively*," I add on, waiting with bated breath for his reaction.

He pulls my neck down and rests his forehead against mine. "There's no way anyone else could captivate my attention the way you have, Pretty Boy. I'd love nothing more."

My chest rumbles with soft laughter, and I close my eyes to soak in this moment before whispering, "Be patient with me. I don't know what to make of everything I'm feeling just yet, but just know I've never felt such conviction for anyone else before."

"Take all the time you need. I'm not going anywhere, Will."

"Thank you."

With everything falling apart around me, Brooks has been my anchor, keeping me grounded when all I want to do is drift away. I'll do my best to give him all the reassurance he needs from here on out.

Speaking in poetry isn't something I'm capable of, so instead, I pull him in and show him how I'm really feeling in the way we communicate best.

21

BROOKS

A Shoe Named Lucy

Six years ago, I missed out on my senior prom. Talia Houseman was the hottest girl in school, and I was the lucky kid who beat out six other guys who asked her.

Eighteen-year-old me loved having the attention of a pretty girl, especially one who every guy in my grade was vying for. Maybe that's where my big head came from.

Talia had a bit of a reputation—one that coined her as "experienced." But that's not why I wanted to go with her. Outside of the whispers around school that Talia Houseman gave the best head in our entire grade, she was actually cool as fuck.

164

She knew about me being bi and didn't care about the mean things guys in our grade would say about me.

"How could Warren like pussy and dick? What a homo."

"Makes sense he's a catcher. Squatting all day long because he likes it up the ass."

"You think Brooks gives head better than Talia Houseman?"

Can't say the words didn't hurt, but I always had baseball to work out my pent up anger toward the puny-brained homophobes at school. But then Talia came along, and I fed off the jealousy from my bullies who wanted her.

With my suit rented and tie that matched her dress bought, I felt on top of the world the day leading up to prom. I had scouts calling my house multiple times a week, and word was getting out that I could possibly be drafted. College or straight to the league?

My opportunities were endless. Senior prom was the cherry on top of all the good things coming my way, and I couldn't wait to dance the whole night with Talia.

As I look into the hotel room mirror, a flash of my eighteen-year-old self stares back at me. Adjusting the bow tie around my neck, a flood of emotions rush through me as an unexpected sting pricks behind my eyes.

"Hey, could you help me with—" Will walks into the bathroom with his head down, fumbling with his bowtie when he stops in his tracks, eyes locked on me through the mirror. "Wow," he says on a heavy breath, slack-jawed.

I try to force a smile, inhaling deeply as I take in Will's handsome face. The custom tuxedo is practically sewed to his body. An absolutely perfect fit. I try not to let the memories from prom night pull me under, but Will's gotten pretty good at reading me with the amount of time we've spent together.

Will leans on the door jamb, his eyes softening then etched with concern when he notices the forced expression in my features. "You alright?"

I turn to face him as I lean back on the bathroom counter, crossing one ankle over the other. Well, I can't avoid it now. I've exposed myself, and I can't find it in me to lie to Will or avoid the truth. Seeing him all dressed up—handsome as the day I first laid eyes on him—has me wanting to share every detail of my life, even if it's painful to bring up.

"I was just thinking about my senior prom," I say quietly.

His eyes light up at that, a grin tipping his lips. "Yeah? Seeing me in a tux got you feeling nostalgic?"

Rubbing the back of my neck, I exhale, trying not to fight the memories from that time in my life. "Seeing you in that tux makes me wish I made it to prom," I murmur, clearing my throat when the words catch. "Sorry. Just . . . random shit from my past popping up at the worst times. I don't wanna ruin the night before it even starts."

Will pushes himself off the door jamb and steps into my space, caging me in against the sink. His nose brushes mine, his cologne wrapping around me as the soft scrape of his stubble grazes my cheek. I gain a strange sort of comfort with his scent and his proximity, coaxing me to share more before he asks for it.

I tell Will about Talia and the boys in my class who wanted her. I tell him about the shit they'd say and rumors they'd spread about me—all because a popular girl from school wanted to go to prom with me.

The baseball playing fag.

"The night before prom, I got a text from one of the guys who bullied me, inviting me to a guys' night since we were all gonna be in the same group."

Will listens intently, his thumb softly brushing over my hand in slow, grounding circles. I swallow hard, his touch keeping me steady as he nods for me to go on. "I was just a kid, you know? I wanted to be accepted. I thought his invitation was a sort of olive branch. So, I said yes."

"And then?"

I sigh, closing my eyes as if the memory from that night hurts too much. Probably because it does, even though I hate to admit it. "I showed up with a case of beer I stole from my dad, thinking that would somehow make me cooler or something. I didn't even make it through the front door until I was lights out, flat on my ass in the front yard."

Will's jaw tightens, anger flaring across his face. "What?" he grits through clenched teeth.

"They jumped me. Beat me to a pulp. A neighbor who was walking his dog ended up finding me face down in the grass. He called 911."

"Fuck, baby," Will whispers, rolling his forehead against mine. "I'm so fucking sorry that happened to you."

I shrug a shoulder, trying for nonchalance, but the ache in my chest betrays me. Phantom pain shoots through my ribs at the memory of them being kicked repeatedly.

"It's in the past," I murmur. "I came out stronger. Since we were eighteen, they were charged as adults. I pressed charges. They went to jail, and I became a professional ball player."

A small grin tugs on my lips as I meet his eyes with adoration. "And now I get to call the hottest pitcher in the league *mine.* Safe to say I won at life, Sin."

Nothing beats seeing Will blush. His cheeks tint pink, and the hint of a smile threatens to graze those full lips I love to take. Lips I'm two seconds away from tasting because I fucking can.

As if he read my mind, we collide in a deep kiss, one full of longing. I feel his empathy for me and the journey I've been on to get me where I am today.

I'm proud to be queer and no longer let the ghosts of my pasts define me. When Will's tongue tangles with mine, I taste a future that I never saw for myself.

A house. A family. And Will Sinclair.

Holy shit.

A live band plays an upbeat tune as the crowd of people swells by the second. My eyes widen at the insanity of it all. Although this is more of Will's scene, he seems just as awestruck as me. Probably because his eyes land on a portrait of a little girl with a smile from ear to ear.

She's blonde like Will, has a face like Will, and from a picture alone—I can tell has a heart like Will.

Abigail.

"She's beautiful. I see so much of you in her," I muse.

His eyes never leave the gold framed photo, his navy gaze welling with unshed tears and a faint, aching smile. "She is—was," he chokes out.

"Is," I correct softly.

He nods. "Yeah. Is."

When his eyes finally meet mine, the urge to kiss him pulses through me. I know I'm here as his date, but I let him set the pace. Coming out and landing a fat one in front of his family and former organization probably isn't the right move tonight.

"William!" Jameson Sinclair's voice cuts through the bustling crowd.

I brace for an awkward reunion, but instead, Will's face breaks open with relief as he pulls his father into a tight hug.

His beautiful mother stands beside the two of them in a long satin gown with one of those scarf thingies wrapped around her shoulders. She looks every bit the part of the elegant wife of a team owner.

When Will finishes greeting his parents, his hand lands on my lower back, nudging me closer. "Mom, Dad, this is Brooks Warren. My date tonight," Will says with pride in his voice.

Fucking butterflies flap around in my empty stomach, wishing now that I ate something before this thing because meeting Will's parents actually has me nervous. But I roll my shoulders back, offering my hand for his father first, then his mother.

"Mr. and Mrs. Sinclair, it's an honor to meet you."

"It's very nice to meet you too, Brooks. Please, call me Jameson. And this is my wife, Anne."

"You look lovely, sweetheart," Anne says sweetly.

"Thank you, ma'am. Can't show up on this man's arm looking anything short of worthy."

That gets a genuine laugh from Will's parents, and I inwardly high-five myself that my charm works on not just one Sinclair, but three.

"Laying it on thick, eh, War?" Will mumbles in my ear.

I fight a smile, leaning closer to him and whispering, "Gotta impress my future in-laws."

If I could take a picture in real-time of Will's face right now, I'd keep it in my back pocket at all times in case I ever needed a laugh. "I'm kidding, Sin. The wedding bells aren't ringing just yet," I tease. "But I love watching you squirm. Once a stiff, always a stiff."

"I'll give you something stiff, alright," Will growls, his voice low and dripping with lust.

Is he hard beneath those Armani pants? I know I fucking am.

"Hey, brother." A tall brunette man with striking Sinclair genes approaches, holding out his hand to Will.

"Dawson. It's been a while. Good to see you."

Will's tone is borderline icy, and it's not exactly the sibling warmth I'm used to when I see Jade. The many layers of Will seem to surface, and I find myself pulling them back little by little to get the whole story.

"You too. Brooks Warren?" Dawson addresses me, shaking my hand. "Dawson Sinclair. I hope my brother is good company."

With a firm handshake, I give him a full smile. "He sure is. It's nice to meet you."

"I'm gonna grab a drink. You two want anything?"

Will answers for both of us, shaking his head. "No, that's okay. We'll get something later. Go make your rounds," he clips.

Dawson says nothing, giving us a polite nod as he walks away. I'll have to circle back to that another day. The tension in Will's shoulders is still there, and I ache to rub them out. It's killing me that I can't just reach out and touch him the way I want.

The last thing I want is for Will to see me being needy or to talk his ear off about my observations, so I shove my hands into my suit pants pockets and follow his lead.

"Son, make sure you go and say hello to the sponsors. We'll catch up with you two later," Jameson adds, whisking Anne away with him.

"Sorry," he grumbles. "I know it's a lot, but I'm so damn glad you're here with me."

My heart beats faster. "It's fine. I'm happy to meet your family. They're nice."

He snorts, leading me toward a table with what looks like yellow roses. "We're fucked up. But what family isn't? All that matters is that I have you, and you have me."

Now that we're closer to the table lined with a black tablecloth, I see the yellow roses are tied with orange satin ribbons with pins.

"What's all this?" I ask, picking up a rose.

I prick my finger on a pin by accident, a small bead of blood swelling on my thumb. Without thinking, Will immediately takes my thumb, sucking the blood off my finger. I'm too shocked to pull back, watching him with hooded eyes as he stares at me with the same amount of lust.

He coolly pops my thumb out of his mouth, smirking.

"Um . . . thanks?" I say awkwardly, willing the flag pole in my pants to chill out.

Will picks up the flower that pricked me off the table, presenting it to me like an offering. "This is a boutonniere. The flower is yellow to represent childhood cancer, and the orange ribbon is for leukemia awareness." His jaw clenches, fingers slightly shaking. "Typically, for prom, your date presents you with one of these to pin on your lapel. So, um . . ." Will stammers, and it's the most adorable fucking thing I've ever witnessed.

"Sinclair," I whisper, leaning in close. "Are you asking me to the prom?"

I wish Will's smile could cure cancer so that Abigail could see how amazing her big brother is. With trembling hands, he bites his lip as he pins the boutonniere to my lapel, both of us smiling like a pair of lovesick fools.

"Can I put one on you, too?"

Will nods, and I follow suit. Once we both have our boutonnieres on, a photographer approaches us. "Picture for the paper, Mr. Sinclair?"

I immediately look to Will to gauge his response. Last time we were photographed, his world exploded, and I was there to pick up the pieces. Though, he should know by now that if the world was ending, I'd never leave his side.

Fully expecting him to tell this guy to fuck off, he does the opposite and pulls me in close, flush to his hip.

The photographer seems shocked himself, readying his camera that's strapped around his neck with a cheeky smile.

"Okay! Big smiles now!"

Will's arm wraps possessively around my waist, and I couldn't fake the smile on my face even if I tried. The flash nearly blinds me, but Will's professional and polite, shaking the photographer's hand.

He disappears back into the crowd, and Will's gaze lands back on mine.

"You sure you're okay with him printing that?" I ask, hesitance lacing my voice.

It's not that I'm not confident in my relationship with Will—it's just I don't want him to bite off more than he can chew. I know we're not making out in the middle of the gala for everyone to see, but he's looking at me like he wants to eat me alive and putting his arm around my waist like I'm no one else's but his.

He's introduced me as his date, and I've met his family, and—fuck. I hate feeling like the other shoe might drop. Being on Will's arm gives me a high that no drug could ever provide. He's pure, unfiltered—a straight shot in my veins.

"Of course I'm sure," he answers with confidence. "Let them say what they will. Because I know exactly what I want." His voice drops an octave, and I'm not sure how much longer I can hold out with these heated stares and the gravelly timbre of his voice literally vibrating my skin.

"Yeah? And what's that, Sin?" I whisper in his ear.

"I want—"

"Will? Oh my god. It's really you."

Both of our heads snap toward the honey-like voice, and a slender blonde with legs for days walks toward us. When I watch Will's face fall and his body tense, I think I might have manifested what I was dreading just moments ago.

"Lucy," Will rushes out on an exhale.

"Lu—" I start, but I'm cut off when she slams her body straight into my man's arms.

In a delayed reaction, Will's eyes widen with shock as she melts into him. But when he wraps his arms around her like he's done it a thousand times before, I hate how hard my heart bottoms out, leaving me in a pile of doubt.

The other shoe might be dropping, and her name is Lucy.

WILLIAM

Quite the First Impression

"Lucy, what are you doing here?" I ask, though it's pointless because I know what she's doing here. Her parents are good friends with mine, and I'm pretty sure they haven't missed a single gala since the inaugural one nearly twenty years ago.

"Well, other than the fact that I wanted to support your family, I also selfishly hoped I'd run into you," she admits, sighing in contentment as she breathes me in.

Lucy Astor—or shit, I guess it's Lucy Cromwell now—was once the woman I thought I'd spend the rest of my life with. That is, until she cheated on me with my friend and teammate at the time, Darren Cromwell.

Okay, so maybe we weren't destined to become husband and wife, but our parents sure were set on the two of us ending up together.

We were high school sweethearts, and she was beside me when my name was called for the draft. She even went to college at UPenn when I was drafted by Philadelphia. Fast forward to my second season with the team when I came back to our shared apartment early from a pitching practice to find Lucy riding my third baseman in our bed.

Looking back on it, the betrayal hurt far more than the fact that I'd lost her. Lucy and I were good friends, and we shared a few years of memories together, so that part was hard. But the fact that I was cheated on by someone I had trusted hurt the most.

Of course, the last time I talked to her, she had blamed me for being distant and never opening up to her. What I can realize now looking back on things was I never really focused on anything outside of baseball and the physical release our relationship provided me. She was right to resent me for keeping my walls up with her. Still doesn't excuse the betrayal from her and my former friend, though.

I'm pulled back to the present when I look over Lucy's shoulder to find Brooks wearing a forlorn frown. Stepping out of Lucy's embrace, I try to excuse myself, but before I can, she pouts her bottom lip out. "I was so upset when you didn't show up to the wedding."

The wedding. As in her wedding. To Darren. Is she really that obtuse to the situation?

My eyebrows shoot to my forehead. "Really?" I ask through a chuckle before I can stop myself.

"Yes, really. I never imagined you'd miss my wedding day. In fact, there was a period of my life where I thought you'd be the one I'd marry."

"Well, it turns out that everything worked out for the both of us in the end. We're both happy now, and that's all that matters."

Lucy opens her mouth to say something, but she stops when I pull Brooks flush to my hip. He places his hand on my lower back in a way that instantly soothes me.

My ex doesn't miss the gesture, her eyes zeroing in on where our bodies connect. "So the rumors are true? You're . . . gay?"

"No, I'm his," I correct, causing both Lucy and Brooks to straighten in surprise.

"Now, if you'll excuse us, I'd like to dance with my date," I tell her, grabbing Brooks' hand and leading him out onto the dance floor where the band has just started playing. Leaving him standing off to the side, I go up to a member of the band and make a song request.

As I make my way back to Brooks, I grab his hand in mine and ask, "May I have this dance?"

Brooks' cheeks heat in the most adorably bashful way. "You sure?"

"I've never been more certain," I assure him.

"Should we talk about what just happened back there?"

I shrug. "What's there to talk about? Lucy was my high school girlfriend. We dated until we were twenty, when she cheated on me with my teammate. Honestly, it was for the best. She ended up marrying him, and if not for her cheating, I may have never met you."

"Is that so?" he questions.

"I'm beginning to learn that some things happen for a reason."

"You're damn right they do," he tells me, tugging me toward the dance floor. Just as we make our way onto it, the band plays the opening chords of an acoustic version of "Collide" by Howie Day.

Pulling Brooks into my chest, I grasp his waist with one hand and join our hands with the other.

"Did you pick this song?" he asks in a hushed tone.

"I did. I heard it the other day on the radio and it made me think of us."

"What about it made you think of us?" he questions as we move in circles around the dance floor.

"For starters, I'm quiet, and you made quite the first impression. But really, you came crashing into my life and knocked me off my feet. You took me off guard when your heart collided with mine."

His eyes twinkle as he looks up at me. "Quite the first impression, hmm?"

"Yeah, you really got me with the whole name calling thing."

Brooks chuckles. "I don't know what you're talking about."

"No? What was it you called me again? Oh, yeah, I believe it was 'arrogant, pompous dick.'"

Now he throws his head back and howls. "God"—he hiccups between laughs—"you really were an arrogant, pompous dick at first."

"And now?"

"Now you've become one of my closest friends. Someone I trust entirely. The first person I want to talk to about my day or when anything big or small happens. My sole fixation as I fall asleep and my first thought when I wake."

Warmth I've never felt before spreads through my chest from his words.

Fuck, I'm pretty sure at some point in the past few months, I've fallen inexplicably in love with Brooks Warren.

Just as I'm working up the courage to declare my feelings to him, something catches his attention out of the corner of his eyes.

"Nothing like being fashionably late," he mutters.

"What?"

"Turn around," Brooks tells me, nodding to something behind me.

When I do, I see about a dozen of our teammates filtering into the ballroom.

I whip my head back to Brooks and ask, "What are they doing here?"

His smile lights up his face as he says, "The guys came together to support you. We each came up with items and activities to donate to the auction." Pulling up the sleeve of his tux, he looks down at his black watch and rolls his eyes. "I told Mateo to get them here a half hour ago. I swear the guy is never on time for anything."

Brooks leads me across the room to where several of our teammates are standing in line at the bar.

I shake Mateo's hand and thank him for coming and helping Brooks organize this. Truett cuts in, letting me know he plans to auction a date night with him, and that he hopes a cougar is the winning bidder.

Just as I order drinks for me and Brooks, our head coach and his wife, Quentin and Stormy Hunter, come up behind us in line.

Shaking Coach's hand, I ask, "Can I get you two a drink?"

"Sure, I'll take a scotch, please," Coach requests.

"What about you, Stormy?"

"Oh, I'll just take a club soda, please," she answers, her cheeks heating.

Truett not having a clue when it comes to filters asks, "A club soda? Are congratulations in order, Coach?"

Stormy laughs awkwardly. "Oh, no. Not yet, at least. We're about to start trying though." Hooking her arm through Coach's, she looks up at him and smiles, but if I'm being honest, he looks a bit green. He grabs at his collar, adjusting it in discomfort. His wife doesn't miss the action, and she does a poor job of hiding her frown.

Yikes.

I turn to the bartender and add Coach's drink order.

"Thanks for offering up a week's stay at your ski chalet in Aspen for auction, Coach," Brooks says, shaking his hand.

I reach out and shake his hand as well. "Yes, thank you for being here, Coach. It means a lot to me and my family."

"Our pleasure," Coach answers, placing his hand on the small of Stormy's back.

"Brooksy! I made it!" a feminine voice squeals before a woman slams into Brooks' arms, causing him to stumble back a few steps.

"Jade! About damn time you showed up," he tells her, giving her a kiss on the side of her head as he sets her back on her feet.

"It takes time to look this good," she retorts, stepping back and making a show of waving an arm down her body. Brooks' little sister looks stunning in a deep green, floor-length velvet gown that clings to her curves in ways that has the heads of several of our teammates turning.

"You look stunning," I tell Jade, wrapping my arms around her when she pulls me into a hug.

"Everything looks perfect. Thank you so much for having me come with you guys."

"You're the only plus one I realized the two of us had," I admit.

"He did good, didn't he?" she asks as we both gaze at her brother.

"He did," I agree, a small smile curving the corners of my mouth.

"What are we watching right now?" I lean in and ask Brooks as we stare at the bidding war I just stumbled across after using the restroom.

"One thousand dollars! Do we have fifteen hundred?" The auctioneer looks at Dawson's raised paddle and points. "Fifteen hundred!"

Dawson openly leers at Jade's backside in her form-fitting dress, causing me to curse under my breath.

Brooks narrows his eyes at my little brother and then mutters, "I swear to God, I'll kill him if he so much as looks at my baby sister again like that."

I throw my head back and laugh. "Oh, come on. Daws is relatively harmless."

A guffaw escapes him, and I scratch my head. "What I'm confused about is why he's bidding on Jade's month of hot yoga instruction when he clearly lives here and not San Diego."

"Two thousand! How about three? Can we get three?"

"And I'm confused why Mateo would have a death wish. What is he thinking, bidding on these private sessions with Jade?" he turns to ask me.

"Three thousand! Can we get thirty-five hundred?" The auctioneer pauses, looking around the room. "Three thousand, going once, twice, sold!"

Leaning down, I place my hand on Brooks' shoulder and ask, "Did you know about this?"

"About Jade auctioning off a month's worth of her hot yoga sessions that I had no idea she taught? No, can't say I did," he huffs, crossing his arms.

"What's got you more upset right now? The fact that Mateo won the bid and will have alone time with her or the fact that you didn't know something about your baby sis?"

"Both," he grumbles.

He's so fucking adorable right now. All worked up like someone pissed in his cereal. God, I'm starting to sound like him even in my own head. What's gotten into me?

Brooks turns his head and fixes his gaze on me. As I stare into his mossy eyes, the rest of the ballroom fades away. My heart is filled with adoration for all the work he put in to get the team here to surprise me and add to the auction.

He gave me time to open up to him about Abigail, honing in on his patience. I've never felt such pure, unadulterated love for someone else before. And I think it's time I show him just exactly where my feelings stand.

Dipping my head, I whisper into his ear, "Perhaps I could help you take your mind off things?"

Brooks smirks. "Oh yeah? How do you plan on doing that?"

"My parents offered for us to stay at their place tonight. Did I mention my childhood bedroom is on the opposite wing as my parents' bedroom?"

He rocks back on his heels. "That's a shame. I was hoping we'd get to role play like we're back in high school and try to keep quiet while I made you come."

"I prefer to hear every whimper and moan you give me," I hum in his ear, nipping at the lobe before pulling away and subtly adjusting myself.

"Let's go," Brooks growls out, grabbing my hand and making his way toward the exit.

"I'm going to give you the prom night of your dreams, baby."

BROOKS

Love On Top

IT'S PRETTY SURREAL STANDING in the middle of Will's childhood bed-room. Calling it a *bedroom* feels wrong—more like a mini mansion.

"You could get lost in here," I say, turning in a slow circle. "What kid even gets a room this size? This is nuts."

Will chuckles, and the sound does something twisty to my insides, melting me where I stand. "To be honest, I didn't spend much time in here," he says after a beat. "Big house, big room . . ." He pauses, his smile fading just a little. "But it was lonely."

Thinking about our little one-story casita in the lower-class neighborhood gives me a humble pause. I can almost hear Dad's snoring vibrating my bedroom walls or Jade's high-pitched laughter cutting through the house from whatever show she was watching.

Will's life was so different from mine, and I hate myself a little for ever judging him by his status. All this space, all this privilege—and still, loneliness found a way to fill every corner.

Something about that makes me want to take away every trace of loneliness he's ever felt. Things with his parents seem to be improving, but there's still a hollowness in him I ache to fill.

I step closer, sliding my arms around his waist. He exhales, tension melting from his body, like just being near me lightens the weight off his shoulders.

"You're not alone anymore, you know that right? You've got me. Always," I murmur, brushing my cheek against his.

Will only nods, taking my lips in a fierce kiss that steals the breath clear out of my lungs. I gasp, parting my mouth for him as he tangles his tongue with mine.

"Fuck," I rasp, tugging hard on the lapels of his suit jacket.

The kiss deepens with Will slanting his mouth over mine, and his hands work to slide my suit jacket over my shoulders.

"Naked. Now," Will growls into my mouth.

We're a mess of frantic hands and feverish kisses. He fucks my mouth with his tongue like it's his mission to make me blow my load before he's even really touched me. I'm so hard it hurts, my dick throbbing with each item of clothing he sheds off my body.

My fingers struggle to unbutton his shirt, and in his impatience, Will rips it open with buttons flying all over the place.

Belts come off, shoes go flying, and next thing I know, my back is shoved up against the wall with his teeth sinking into my neck, hungry and fucking feral.

Our naked chests heave against one another, and the thunderous thud of his heart keeps me in this moment with him. I taste the inside of his mouth, craving other parts of him on my tongue. His cock presses against mine, hot and leaking already from the tip.

I start to sink to my knees until Will's hands grip my shoulders, stopping me cold.

"Wait," he grits out, panting like he just ran a marathon. "I . . . Fuck, how do I say this," he mumbles, shaking his head back and forth.

The sight of him flustered, cheeks tinged pink, makes me grin. I cup his face, thumbs brushing his jaw. "Hey. Just tell me."

"Brooks . . ." He almost looks pained as he rubs a fist over his chest.

My smile falters. Panic flickers in my chest as I search his face. "What's wrong? What is it?"

Time slows down when Will pierces me with those navy eyes. They shine with the moonlight pouring in from the massive windows, and I can see they're filled with a reverence that has my heart skipping. Everything around us fades to black, and my vision tunnels with Will at the center of it all.

"I don't ever want to lose you," he says with our foreheads pressed together.

"You won't, Will. I told you I'm not going anywhere."

He exhales a shaky laugh. "No, I know. It's just—shit, I'm terrible at this." His mouth quirks into a disbelieving smile. "I think I love you."

The words rush out of him, but they hit me in slow motion. I'm pretty sure my heart stops. My lungs forget how to function. Did he just say what I think he said? Will *The Pretty Boy Stiff* Sinclair loves *me?*

A stunned laugh slips out before I can stop it, spreading into a grin that feels too big for my face. "You *think* you love me, Sin?"

His lips brush mine, and that small touch alone sends an electric current throughout my entire body. I'm on fire, but his confession only makes me burn hotter.

"Let me try that again," Will whispers, tasting the edge of my smile as he kisses me deeper. "I *know* I'm in love with you. And I know there's no one else I want but *you.*"

"Yeah?" My legs are close to giving out, knees turning to jelly, but Will pins me in place with not only his hands but now—his heart.

Who would've thought.

"Yeah," he murmurs, kissing me with so much force I groan into his mouth with how good it feels to have him take me the way he wants. The way he can anytime, anywhere.

Will Sinclair fucking loves me!

And the thing is, I love him, too. I've known it for a while now, but hearing him say it out loud settles something inside me that has all the pieces falling into place the way it was always supposed to.

I reach down and stroke his thick length in my hand, rolling my thumb over the wetness seeping out of his tip. The hiss that escapes his mouth goes straight to my cock that hangs heavy, begging to be touched, sucked, and fucked.

We're moving across the room, our lips never once leaving each other. We fall down on his bed, the scent of clean linen and something that's so Will overtaking my senses.

I land on top of him, shamelessly grinding myself over his length as my hands thread through his hair. Will's hands find the firm muscle on my ass, kneading and spreading my cheeks apart. His finger teases my hole, grazing over it in tortuous circles.

As much as I want him to plunge his thick fingers inside me, my body is overcome with the need to taste him. Reaching around my back and gripping his wrist, I stop him, then kiss my way down his body.

I take a nipple between my teeth and smile when he makes a noise between pleasure and pain. I circle it with my tongue to soothe the sting, then lick and kiss further south, lapping up the trail of precum left on his washboard abs.

Without warning, I take him deep to the back of my throat while my insides rattle with arousal as his cock pulses more precum into my mouth.

"Goddamn, that's fucking good," Will grits. "Don't stop."

And I don't stop—not for a minute. He fucks my throat like a man on the loose, wild and untamed in every sense. Spit dribbles out the corner of my mouth, slowly dripping toward his ass. My finger finds it, wetting his tight hole with my saliva and nudging the tip of my finger inside.

"Oh, fuck yes. More, baby."

I pop off his cock with one finger in his ass, then push his legs back to expose himself more to me. Leaning forward, I let saliva pool in my mouth before spitting it raw onto his hole.

"Jesus fucking Christ, War. Get me wet."

I spit again, my cock pulsing when he moans loud into the room, head tilted back like I'm about to ruin him and he's giving me full permission to do it. My finger pushes deeper, and Will grunts with ragged breaths the more I give him.

One more finger. And another.

"Want more, Sinclair?"

Our gazes lock on each other, his pupils blown and full lips parted. I can't help but take his mouth again, nipping and sucking his sexy fucking pout.

"I . . . I need more. Please. I'm ready," he rasps against my lips, his voice husky and laced with want.

I lift an eyebrow. "Ready? For what, Sin?"

I have an idea, but I want to hear him say it. *I need to hear him say it.* If he's wanting what I'm dying to give him, get me on a bullet train straight to fucking euphoria because that's where I hope this is heading.

Will roughly swallows, the bob of his Adam's apple mesmerizing me. *Fuck.* Even the way his throat works has me coming undone, and he doesn't even have to touch me.

"Go to my bag there." He nods his chin over toward his duffle by the door. "Bring what's in the side pocket. Hurry."

Will Sinclair has surprises up his sleeve, does he? Full body tingles erupt all over my skin, and I'm frantically sprinting off the bed and toward his bag so we don't waste a minute we can be together.

When I unzip the side pocket, I find what Will asked me to get.

Lube.

Hurrying back, I straddle his thighs, dangling the lube over him with a cheeky smirk on my face. "You wanna fuck me, Sin?"

He shakes his head no, but there's not a hint of amusement on his face. "You know that's not what I want right now, War."

"Say it then."

I uncap the lube with a snap, keeping my wanton gaze on Will. Pouring a generous amount on my fingers, I work to stretch him again, plunging into his tightness with two fingers.

He hisses, biting his bottom lip. But the way his rock-hard cock throbs and pulses out beads of precum tells me he loves the way I work his ass.

"I'm waiting," I taunt, adding a third finger.

"Fuck me," he growls.

"Say it again."

"Fuck. Me."

"Again," I demand, grazing his prostate with the pads of my fingers.

"Fuck me, Brooks. Give me your cock in my ass right the fuck now!"

His impatience spurs me on, a dark, low chuckle vibrating from deep within my chest. Keeping my fingers inside him, I lean down to whisper into his mouth.

"I've been dreaming about this, Sin. I'll make it so fucking good for you. I swear it."

"I know you will, baby. I know."

I press a sweet kiss to his lips, then slowly pull my fingers out of him. Will keeps his legs spread wide for me, and the sight of his tight hole makes my mouth water and my balls heavy.

I can't believe I'm about to bury myself inside of him. Something I've thought of more times than I'd like to admit. Every shower session, late night jerk, and the cause of my early morning wood leads to *Sin* personified.

Pouring lube all over my cock, I stroke myself a few times as I stare down at Will with love in my eyes.

Love and lust, desire and need—no matter what emotions pass through them, they will always belong to him.

"I'll go slow, okay? I'm gonna stretch you a bit more," I tell him as I press the tip of my dick to his ass.

Will nods, hands gripping his sheets.

Pushing the tip of me an inch at a time, Will's eyes widen as he watches me disappear into him."Holy shit," he marvels.

"You're doing so good, Sin. Relax for me. Let me in."

When I push a little deeper, I feel him tense. I stop, letting him accommodate my size. "Stroke yourself. It'll help you relax."

Compliancy is sexy on Will. Rarely does he ever do what I say, but when he does, I eat it up like a fucking dog. His hand grips his shaft, throbbing and hot as he strokes himself slowly from root to tip.

"That's it," I murmur, feeding him more of my inches.

"Oh, holy fuck, baby," Will moans out.

Finally, my entire length is inside him, pulsing with the ravenous need to rut into him. "Shit, you feel so fucking good, Sin. So fucking good."

"Move," Will demands. "I need you to move."

My mind takes mental snapshots of Will on his back with his strong legs spread wide, fat cock heavy in his hand with my dick in his ass. What a goddamn vision it is.

When my eyes have their fill, I fucking move. I pull back, then thrust home—a beautiful, broken cry leaving Will's lips.

I fuck him mad, my cock slick with lube and arousal as I rut like a wild animal in heat. In and out. Over and over. Again and again and again.

"Damn, you feel so good, Sin. Your tight ass is taking me so damn well. I don't wanna stop," I praise.

Will's so lost in pleasure, he can't speak. He can't think. He can't breathe. He's choking on his words, and the primal beast in me craves it—craves giving him more of me so his body, mind, and soul have no choice but to surrender to me.

I'm barely hanging on by a thread with the way his ass grips me like an iron fist, squeezing the head of my cock with each thrust. When the tingles spread throughout my groin, I have to dig deep to find the willpower to keep myself from blowing too early.

Will's eyes squeeze shut, face twisted in wicked pleasure as I fuck him with reckless abandon. "Nuh-uh, open your eyes. Look at me, Sin."

Navy eyes fly open and turn black with arousal. Will's breathing stutters. His chest seizes. His hands find their way to the outside of my thighs, squeezing so hard I hope they bruise in the morning so I'll have physical evidence of this man and his desire for me.

The veins on his gorgeous cock strain as I fuck his ass, and I'm seconds away from unleashing a violent orgasm inside him.

Hold out, Warren.

"Oh, my god." Will's low moan reverberates from his chest, his eyes struggling to stay locked on me. But the way his mouth parts and his ass squeezes me tells me he's on the precipice of a release that I'm begging for.

"Give it to me, Sin. Come for me."

Slamming my hips hard into his ass, the first thick rope of cum spurts from him, shooting so far it hits the masculine column of his throat. It's by far the hottest fucking thing I've ever witnessed, and I watch in awe as he growls out his release without even touching himself.

"Holy fucking shit, Sin. Keep going, baby, goddamn."

Will's grunts and moans push me over the edge as I find my release, shooting my load so deep in his ass he could taste it for days.

"Fuck!" I shout with a roar, stuttering my hips into him as I come over and over.

Explosions of white cloud my vision, and I'm falling so deep into the throes of euphoric release that it has me struggling to stay upright. The weight of my orgasm threatens to knock me down, but I grip Will's thighs harder in my hands as I thrust every last drop of my cum inside of him.

Endless stripes of Will's cum paint his slick abs. My body gives out, and I fall on top of him, out of breath. My vision is spotty, having just come the hardest I have in my fucking life.

Will's breaths are heavy against my chest, and I look up to see some of his release dripping from his sharp jaw. I lick it up, tasting him on my tongue.

My cock still throbs inside him with every bit of his cum I lap from his jaw and throat.

"Will," I breathe out, claiming his lips once more. "Taste that? That's me making you fucking mine."

Will's hands find my hair, threading his fingers through the dark strands. His breathy chuckle is an instant shot of arousal to my cock again, and it wants to stir to life while still buried deep in his ass.

"I'm fucking yours, baby. All yours," he says, then moves his hands to grip my ass. "And you're all mine."

Our chests stick together from his release, but I don't care to move or to take any weight off him. He's not complaining, so neither am I. Will's mouth seeks mine, and we kiss for what feels like hours, sweaty and sticky from intense love-making.

That's exactly what we did. Made love. The way our eyes stayed connected, saying everything our mouths couldn't because of the immense pleasure coursing through us. Being inside of Will was more than claiming a part of him that no one has had before. It was sealing a promise between us—something wholly us and sacred that no one else would understand.

Not that I'd need them to. The only two people in the world who could get me and Will Sinclair are . . . well . . . me and Will Sinclair. Rightfully so. Fuck everyone else.

Fuck all the people who look at us and think the worst.

Fuck the media and their headlines, judging us because we choose to love each other.

And fuck any person who would ever think to come between us, because now that we have each other?

We're untouchable.

"Baby?" Will whispers, pulling back just enough for our breaths to mix.

"Yeah?"

"Move in with me." A statement—no. A demand. Not a question.

Very on brand for William Sinclair.

Two options.

Option one: I can say yes right away, because who am I kidding? Of course I'll say yes. I love this man with everything I have.

Option two: Fuck with him a little and make him sweat, because who am I kidding again? I love doing that almost as much as I love *him.*

A grin pulls at my lips as I suck his tongue back into my mouth, earning that low, sinful sound that makes me want to start all over again.

And because I'm a *fucking brat* according to Pretty Boy himself, I pull back from our kiss, look him straight in the eye, and give him my answer with my entire soul.

"Make me."

EPILOGUE

WILLIAM - DON'T YOU DARE

Three Months Later

"WHAT'S THIS?" BROOKS ASKS when I stand from the edge of our bed to hand him a gift bag.

With rapt attention, I watch the droplets of water as they trail down his broad, tanned chest until they disappear into the towel wrapped around his waist. Clearing my throat, I tell him, "Just a little something that made me think of you. Open it."

He tosses the tissue paper aside and picks up the brown apron I stumbled across online.

His smile transforms from bashful to salacious in seconds. "Mmm, yeah stuff me so hard?" he questions as he reads what's written across the front of the apron.

I try and fail to bite back my chuckle. "Do you like it?"

"What exactly about this made you think of me? Was it the turkey with its legs spread open and stuffing spilling out of it, or just the fact that I love when you stuff me full of your cock?" He quirks a brow, causing him to look downright mischievous.

"Definitely the second one."

"You're starting to sound like me," he points out.

Shit, I really am.

"And you'd be right; I do love being stuffed full of your cock. But I can't wear this today. Our parents will lose their shit."

"Oh, come on. Since when did you become the reserved one in our relationship?" I quip.

"Since you invited your parents and your brother to stay with us for Thanksgiving and proceeded to rant and rave about how great of a cook I am when I've never prepared a Thanksgiving meal for nine people."

That catches my attention. "Nine?"

"Yeah, Mateo was telling me how he was planning on eating a frozen pizza today all by himself, and I couldn't accept the fact that he wouldn't just join us when we're a few houses down the beach."

"Hmm," I hum, wrapping my arms around his waist and dropping a kiss on his exposed collarbone. "Is the almighty War going soft on me?"

Brooks grinds his towel-covered length against me. "Never soft around you."

I shake my head at his antics. "You're incorrigible."

He bites my bottom lip before sucking it into his mouth."Says the man who wants his boyfriend to wear an apron so inappropriate it would surely make his mother clutch her pearls."

"Mom only wears her pearls on Christmas and at weddings," I retort.

"Ah, shit. When we told your family to dress casual, are they going to dress, like, normal people casual or your version of casual? Do I need to call Jade and my parents?"

As if he just realized I was already dressed, he steps back and appraises my outfit. His slow perusal feels as if he's caressing me with his gaze.

"I'll be damned. Casual. And, fuck, only you could make a sweater and dark-washed jeans look this hot." Stepping forward again, he grips hold of my sweater and tugs me impossibly closer.

I love when he pulls me to his chest like this, as if he can't stand for there to be a millimeter of space between us for any length of time. Surprisingly, living with Brooks has gone better than I could've imagined. After being a perpetual bachelor for thirty-four years, I anticipated that it would take time to get used to having someone else in my space. I've never been so happy to have guessed wrong.

"We've got twenty minutes before I need to baste the turkey again. But I bet I can make you come in five," he taunts, adding a cocksure smile for good measure.

"Why waste precious minutes by rushing? If the turkey burns, it burns." I shrug my shoulders before leaning in to capture his lips.

Brooks steps back and rushes his palm up to cover my lips. "Take it back!" he shouts, sounding irrational, bordering on insane.

When I don't say anything, he puts his hands on his hips. "Take it back right now or take your bad energy outta the house before I actually burn the fuckin' turkey."

"You're crazy."

"Yeah? Well, you're crazy for *me*. So I guess we're a couple of nut jobs cohabitating."

I let out a sigh of impatience. "Shut the fuck up and kiss me, baby," I command, pulling him in and taking his lips before he can spew any other insanity.

Just as I place the sweet potato casserole on the dining table, my brother comes sauntering down the stairs with the most arrogant smile on his face.

He can be such a pompous little prick sometimes.

Shit, isn't that exactly how Brooks thought of me when we first met nearly six months ago?

Also, how has it only been six months since we first met? It feels like a lifetime ago yet as if it were only yesterday at the same time. I'm stunned by how quickly I fell for Brooks, and it appears I'm not the only one.

My parents are too thrilled that I've found someone to share my life with to be shocked. No, the skepticism lies squarely on my little brother's shoulders.

Speak of the devil and he shall appear.

"Oh, look. Brooks is over there making googly eyes at you from across the room. How pathetically romantic," he mock-coos.

Again, pompous prick.

"They're moony eyes," I correct in a cool tone.

"Whatever that means." Dawson lets out a deep sigh, turning his back to Brooks. "Doesn't it get tiring having someone so much younger than you to look after all the time?"

I feather my jaw in an attempt to bite back the vitriol I'd love to spray in his face, but ultimately the ugly side only Dawson seems to bring out of me rears its ugly head.

Fisting my hands, I grit out, "You'd think as my baby brother you'd be ecstatic that I've finally found someone I want to spend my life with. Someone who makes me genuinely happy. Instead, you've done nothing but be hypercritical of everything to do with the man I love. What is wrong with you?"

"First of all, I'd hardly consider myself your baby brother anymore now that I'm a thirty-year-old grown man—"

"Debatable as to whether or not you're grown," I retort, cutting him off.

Dawson narrows his eyes. "Second, absolutely nothing is wrong with me. It's *you* I have a problem with."

Before I can even attempt to delve deeper into that discussion, my mom thankfully interrupts us.

"White or red?" she asks, holding up two bottles of wine.

Clearing my throat to give myself a moment of mental transition from whatever the hell that was, I reply, "How about both. I know you prefer white, but Elena prefers red. That bottle there is the one she brought—it's Agiorgitiko, a popular red in Greece. There's also a bottle of Moscato chilling in the wine fridge for Jade if you wouldn't mind grabbing it."

"Ah, Jade's here? I haven't seen her yet. She's so lovely."

My brow furrows in confusion. "You haven't seen her yet? She got here before you did. Hmm. I'll have to see if Brooks can find her."

"No need. I'll go look for her while I grab the bottle of Moscato," Dawson offers, and I'm thankful for the excuse to cut our conversation short. Tonight is definitely not the night to dive deep into the complexities of our sibling issues.

"I was happy to hear your team made it past the first round of playoffs. That's a first in franchise history for the Rays, right?" my mother questions once Dawson heads back upstairs.

My mood sours a bit further, thinking of how our season came to a close. Sure, I should be happy that we managed to turn the team of degenerates into a playoff contender, but I'm still pissed we lost in the second round of playoffs.

Who knows, next season could be my last, and I would do just about anything to be there when Brooks wins his first World Series. To be on the field with him as confetti rains down all around us. I'm going to do everything in my power to help our teammates make the most of our offseason so we can come back stronger than ever next season.

A warm hand envelopes mine, and I look over to find Brooks already smiling at me. My chest warms as my pulse steadies.

No matter if it's something small like being reminded of our losing season, or something as monumental as being outed in front of the world, he is my steadying force—my calm in the storm.

"We're proud of how this season ended up, considering the rough start. I'm looking forward to next season; but I won't lie—my main focus is soaking up as much time getting to know your son in the offseason," Brooks tells my mom.

My mom stares back at him with heart eyes, and for the first time I get a taste of what others possibly see when I look at him, too.

He has her wrapped around his finger, and he knows it.

Cocky little shit.

But I'll take it. The fact that my parents have welcomed him with open arms and embraced my relationship with a man is something I'm feeling incredibly grateful for this Thanksgiving.

"Alright, I think it's time to eat," Brooks announces to everyone.

After we've all taken our seats, passed around food, and filled our plates, the room fills with conversation.

Brooks places his hand over mine and squeezes it, causing my lips to pull into a soft smile. His eyes lift to his little sister sitting across from him, currently eating the potatoes off her plate like there's no tomorrow.

"Jesus, Jade. Could you have some manners and slow the hell down? You're eating like a baby elephant."

I cover my hand to smother a laugh as Jade smiles with her cheeks puffed out full of food. After a couple chews, she swallows before sassily replying to her brother. "I can't help but devour this delicious meal you've prepared for us, big bro." She winks, and Brooks is anything but amused.

"I agree with *pequeña guerra*. This meal is amazing," Mateo adds, shoveling turkey into his mouth.

"What did you just call my sister?" Brooks asks, his voice tight with tension.

"Little War. You know, like a little you." Mateo beams with a cunning smirk.

"Nicknames already, huh?" Dawson mutters behind his wine glass.

My eyes don't know who to look at. Brooks looks like he wants to bite off Mat's head. Jade is eating every item off her plate without a care in the world, and Dawson is saying weird shit and giving side glances toward Jade.

Luckily our parents are all in their own deep conversations, ignoring the strange energy hovering over this end of the table.

Dawson chimes in again, turning to Mateo. "I'm surprised you're still hungry right now. I figured you'd be full from all that dessert you snuck earlier."

Mateo sputters out the wine he just took a swig of.

Dawson shrugs, the gesture innocent enough, but I know better. He's up to no good.

"Dawson," I warn. "Enou—"

"Or maybe it wasn't the two of you I saw sneaking dessert upstairs earlier," he cuts me off, casually cutting into his turkey.

Jade's face heats at the same time as Mateo fists his hands on the table.

What. The. Fuck.

Brooks draws his brows together. "Nah. I just set the pies out. They were untouched, so I'm sure you've got it all wrong."

"Hmm," Dawson hums. "Maybe."

"You *are* wrong," Jade sneers, narrowing her gaze on my brother.

"Yeah, *papi*. Get your eyes checked," Mateo tacks on, pinning Dawson with a glare.

"I'll do that. Oh, before I forget. How'd those hot yoga sessions turn out for you, Costa?"

Mateo eyes him warily, unsure of my brother's motive. I'm feeling the same way, to be honest. Dawson feels like a loose cannon today. Mateo then puts on a performative smile.

"They are good. *Pequeña guerra* is an amazing teacher," he says, casually throwing his arm over her shoulder. "I have one session left."

"Oh, yeah? I bet things are really heating up between the two of you." Dawson waggles his eyebrows before taking a languid sip of wine.

"Don't. You. Dare," Brooks grumbles. But I fear the warning Brooks shoots Mateo's way is too little too late. "Take your arm off my baby sister, you dick."

Eyeing my brother, he looks as if he's about to add fuel to the dumpster fire that's currently happening in front of me. So much for a peaceful first Thanksgiving together.

I turn to face Dawson. "You're done, Daws," I tell him through gritted teeth, but it appears I'm too late by the looks of anger radiating off Brooks in waves.

Oh, fuck. Here we go.

Brooks looks as if he's about to launch himself across the table and wring Mateo's neck. Jade's eyes widen, flicking back and forth between the three men.

Dawson smirks, looking too smug for his own good before taking a bite of turkey. His mouth turns down slightly as he chews. "Turkey's a bit dry, War. Maybe next year."

ACKNOWLEDGMENTS

We would like to thank our husbands—you the real MVPs. No, but seriously, we're so grateful for their love and support while we spent many late nights writing this book together. The solo bedtimes with the kiddos, countless meals to make sure we were fed, their bartending skills to keep us properly hydrated through every spice scene, and booty slaps of encouragement all meant so much, and allowed us to bring this story to life.

A huge shout out to our incredibly talented cover artist, Anya! She is phenomenal to work with and so creative—it was so much fun to watch her take our vision and exceed all of our expectations.

To our editor, Tina: You're a freaking mastermind and we're so grateful for your feedback! We can't wait to continue to work together on the next books in the series.

To Sam & Hannah, our alphas: You both are amazing! Thank you so much for your feedback, for cheering us along as we jumped into this co-writing journey, and for all of your love for Brooks & Will's story. Special shout out to Sam for opening our eyes to the world of MM books!

To Em & Michelle: This book would not be what it is without your incredible feedback. Thank you for taking the time to not only read an extremely rough draft of this book, but to give the most thoughtful, provoking, and respectful feedback for Will and Brooks. We appreciate you both very much!

To Brit, Chelsea, & Sariah: Thank you for your unhinged comments, your enthusiasm for Brooks & Will's story, and your support along the way! Your constant support for both of us as authors means the world to us. Your friendship is everything, and we can't do this journey without y'all! Love you guys so much!

And thank you to every reader and ARC reader who took the time to read our debut co-written story. Many of you have been there for both of us in our own projects from the start, but having you here while Grayce and I achieve a dream of ours together means everything. We look forward to creating more stories together and invite you to never hop off the train with us!

ABOUT THE AUTHORS

Ginsa & Grayce are two millennial, horny bitches who became author besties as they were preparing to release their debut novels in the same summer. After one three-hour FaceTime call and countless deranged texts and DMs later, the San Diego Rays series was born. If you couldn't tell by this author bio how unhinged we really are . . . well now you know after reading Sin & War. We match each other's freaks and never yuck the other's yum. If anything, we yum each other's yum. No kink is outside of our comfort zones. Buckle up, Sin & War was just a glimpse into what's to come.

Follow us on social media @authorginsamichelle @graycerianauthor for updates on all of our projects. Thank you for supporting our journey.

Love,

Ginsa & Grayce

ALSO BY THE AUTHORS

Also by Ginsa Michelle

Oakwood Valley Series

Meet Me in the Vines

(Donovan & Audrey)

Meet Me in the Valley

(Logan & Tia)

Also by Grayce Rian

The Off Ice Series

What It Was

(Griffin & McKenna)

What It Should Be

(Carson & Dakota)

What It Must Be

(Bennett & Scarlett)

What It Could Be

(Jackson & Taevin)